BACK WITH A VENGEANCE

Center Point
Large Print

Also by R. W. Stone and available from
Center Point Large Print:

Badman's Pass
Across the Rio Bravo
Canadian Red

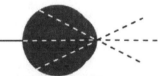

**This Large Print Book carries the
Seal of Approval of N.A.V.H.**

BACK WITH A VENGEANCE

R. W. STONE

CENTER POINT LARGE PRINT
THORNDIKE, MAINE

This Center Point Large Print edition
is published in the year 2019 by arrangement with
Golden West Literary Agency.

First US edition: PublishAmerica

The text of this Large Print edition is unabridged.
In other aspects, this book may vary
from the original edition.
Printed in the United States of America
on permanent paper.
Set in 16-point Times New Roman type.

ISBN: 978-1-64358-100-2 (hardcover)
ISBN: 978-1-64358-104-0 (paperback)

Library of Congress Cataloging-in-Publication Data

Names: Stone, R. W., author.
Title: Back with a vengeance / R.W. Stone.
Description: Center Point Large Print edition. | Thorndike, Maine :
    Center Point Large Print, 2019.
Identifiers: LCCN 2018054971| ISBN 9781643581002 (hardcover :
    alk. paper) | ISBN 9781643581040 (paperback : alk. paper)
Subjects: LCSH: Western stories. | Large type books.
Classification: LCC PS3619.T67 B32 2019 | DDC 813/.6—dc23
LC record available at https://lccn.loc.gov/2018054971

Courage is being scared to death but saddling up anyway

—John Wayne

AUTHOR'S NOTE

Today the West is as much a state of mind as it is a geographic location. It might even be safe to say that for those who believe right will eventually triumph over evil, for those who respect a person more for character than wealth, and for those who will always be young at heart, the West has no boundaries.

The beauty of fiction is that it too has no boundaries, so while there are writers who would describe the West in stark, historically revised, or "politically correct" terms, the author prefers to portray characters from the Old West he enjoyed in his youth.

Sadly there are those who say that heroism is an antiquated or, worse yet, unrealistic concept, and that such portrayals are merely vain attempts to recapture or reinvent past glories. For some unexplained reason such critics feel the need to denigrate any moral or courageous action and frequently ridicule heroic role models.

Some also believe that people who enjoy reading about Westerners who faced great obstacles and triumphed represent a dying breed. I for one think not.

More importantly, I hope not.

There is a good chance the youth of today are

still seeking something noble to believe in, and are truly capable of forming a higher opinion of man's intrinsic worth. Certainly no one can dispute they are in dire need of better role models than those offered by many of the commercially driven, and publicity motivated "stars" of today. I ask you, what better role model is there than the classic American Westerner?

Role models need not necessarily be realistic, but they must be real enough to capture our hearts. They should inspire us and give us hope. Many of us, young and old alike, are tired of the pessimism, fatalism, and negativity that seems to pervade both literature and the audio-visual media of today.

So, to those who long to hear the sound of the cavalry trumpet as brave men charge to the rescue, to those who still believe that help will arrive in the nick of time, and that heroes will prevail, and to all those who simply want a moment's escape to a less complicated or more exciting place and time, this book is dedicated.

BACK WITH A VENGEANCE

CHAPTER ONE

Time is more thought than thing, but it can kill you just the same. The blink of an eye can last an eternity when you are staring at a man whose sole intent is to kill you, and when you finally face death a heartbeat can last forever. More often than not, being alive means fighting to stay alive. Simply put, life is granted to those who want it most.

Despite those fanciful dime novel depictions, a Western face off between two matched and equally determined shootists usually leaves both of them either maimed or dead. So assuming one's not roaring drunk or crazy, the only reason to get into a shoot-out is the sure knowledge that the other fellow isn't as fast or as accurate. Either that, or because you're left with no other choice.

The man opposite me no longer had a way out. Exposed as a thief and a murderer, he suddenly found himself trapped among those he had cheated. All his anger had now turned toward the one person who had spoiled his plans and ruined his future. Unfortunately for me, I was that person. Once he knew that there was nowhere to run, he'd set his mind on making damned sure he took me with him, straight down to hell. So that left both of us with no other options. I wouldn't back down, wasn't about to let him escape, and he sure as shootin' wasn't about to surrender to a hangman's noose.

I knew I wasn't just facing a dangerous man. I was squared off against someone who no longer cared whether he lived or died. That outcome had already been decided for him, the size of the angry crowd forming around us assuring his demise. All he cared about now was revenge. The problem was that I still cared a great deal about what would happen to me.

While it's true that in the past I had managed to survive a couple of shoot-outs unscratched, they'd all been quick battles fought mostly on instinct, reflex, and luck. This one was different. Facing a man head-on in the middle of a street forces you to reflect hard and fast on things. So in the length of a single stride, I came to two conclusions.

The first was that I'd rather die right than live wrong, and the second was that I wasn't quite ready to die, at least not today. The blink of an eye isn't supposed to give you enough time to think all this through, but by the time my right hand had dropped to the grip of my Navy Colt, I'd made my mind up to take whatever he threw my way and to keep on going.

I could actually see the beads of sweat form on his brow and hear the *creak* of his leather holster as his gun hand pulled his Remington free.

Steady now. From somewhere in the back of my mind Pa's words echoed.

Bein' fast don't matter much if you don't hit what you aim at.

I don't truly remember thumbing back the hammer on my Colt, or even drawing it for that matter, but I do remember seeing his gun smoke and hearing the awful blast as the bullet hit me.

Funny, I always thought you couldn't hear the one that finally got you.

The sun perched atop the jagged mountain range and the sky burned a cool orange hue as dusk slowly approached. Down below in the basin the lake reflected a blue so deep it created an aura of peaceful serenity.

Directly across from me and nailed at a slant to the trunk of a large cottonwood was an old slab of wood carved into the shape of an arrow. Scrolled across the center of the weather-beaten sign faded letters spelled out: Blue Lake Ridge, 2 miles.

From that point on, the trail serpentined its way downhill to the basin below, emptying directly into the middle of town. Blue Lake Ridge was situated at the bottom of a narrow gorge where the mountain sloped gradually down into the lakebed. The town was built by its founders on an incline, forming a half circle around the southeast part of the basin. This somewhat unique

13

situation allowed for an unobstructed and rather spectacular view of the lake from almost any part of town.

How such an example of Nature's perfection as the Blue Lake basin could harbor such cruelty and greed will always remain a mystery to me, but of course, back then any thoughts of danger were far from my mind. As I sat astride my palomino stallion staring down into those tranquil waters, that splendid landscape appeared simply to be a patch of pure paradise.

My thoughts were running mostly toward a freshly cooked hot meal, a cold brew, and a soft bunk to stretch out on. The stallion was lathered some from the long uphill ride and his head was hanging a little lower than usual. I was just as bushed as he was, but regardless of how tired and hungry I might be, I know it was inevitable that his needs would be seen to first.

Before my pa died, he'd worked long and hard to obtain true palomino stock, and as a boy I'd helped him breed this particular stallion's line on our ranch back home. Over the years since then, this one horse had carried me long and far without ever so much as a moment's hesitation. A cayuse that game deserved to be stabled, watered, and well grained whenever possible. Pa wouldn't have allowed it any different. He'd trained me early on to warm 'em up goin' out and cool 'em off comin' in. He used to say: *Take care of yourself as well as you take care of your horse and you'll both be happy.* Maybe so, but my horse was usually a lot better off and much happier than I was.

Tied across the back of my old Texas roping saddle were two large saddlebags. The leather was worn down to a shine and one of the buckles was rusting, but it was the contents of those bags that really mattered. There were several pounds of high-grade gold ore packed in each one.

For the past seven months. I had been prospecting in the area up around Bannock City, Idaho. Four of us lived in a couple of patched up Sibley tents and a makeshift cabin that had been thrown together with leftover timber and some floor boards from an old wagon. We shared our claims as we dug and sifted ourselves to exhaustion day after day, often for weeks on end. It's been said that a prospector is nothing more than a cowpoke with his brains knocked out. I wouldn't doubt that for a minute. Out west every prairie dog hole is a gold mine, every hill a mountain, every creek a mighty river, and every prospector a liar if ever there was one.

My friends had been some of the first Pikes Peakers and had come to the area even before John White made a name for himself by striking it big. They had set up camp around Willard Creek, reportedly one of the spots Lewis and Clark had found. To say the place was desolate would be

15

far too complimentary. For one thing the winters were cold enough to freeze horse piss in mid-air, and in summer the place was lousy with grasshoppers. There were so many of the little buggers we had to burn the ground around our tents just to make things livable. We didn't know who the hell this Willard fellow was, and, since we didn't care much, we eventually changed the name to Grasshopper Creek. I thought it was far more appropriate.

Our campsite was one of the most miserably lonely stretches on God's good earth, but the gold we found was almost ninety-nine percent pure, which was fantastic when compared to the ninety-five percent ore found in other territories. It was so rich some folks later took to referring to the whole area as the El Dorado of the north. I don't know much about this El Dorado place, which is supposedly somewhere down south, but to be anything like Grasshopper Creek, it would have to be one cold, wet, and rocky hell-hole.

Some men are born prospectors I guess. They never give up looking under another boulder or sifting the bottom of the next stream. They pitch camp more than a Plains Indian. Such men seem to be eternally optimistic that they will eventually hit the mother lode. For me, prospecting was just a way to earn a little quick cash, and after several months I realized I'd never get any richer than I already was, at least not without the increasingly improbable lucky strike.

Maybe the truth is I was too young and impatient. I didn't want to wait around any longer, just hoping to hit. I guess I didn't have the stick-to-it-tiveness the others had for ground digging, or the instinct to smell out gold ore. Although I had enough glitter to satisfy my immediate needs, most of what I'd dug up or panned came from following the leads of others, not because of any natural ability of my own.

Jeff MacNee, Ross Evans, and Jock O'Reilly had been solid friends. Those men had real sand and taught me a lot. They didn't have to allow me into their camp when I first arrived but instead they had all taken pity on a young loner. I was truly sorry to have to part company with them, but I'd dug up enough color to support me a good while and was anxious to get back out on the trail. It's sort of like an itch you get from time to time, one you gotta scratch. I'd finally realized it was time for me to move on.

A few weeks after leaving camp, I received a letter from my sister Judith. Originally it had arrived in Bannock, where it was later picked up by Jeff. He in turn gave it to a friend of his, Blacky Simmons, who then crossed my trail and passed it off. I hadn't seen her since my seventeenth birthday, but Sis had a special knack for tracking me down by mail every now and then. How she managed it was beyond me, since I never was one for sending back detailed letters.

Even though I didn't write much, I still loved her dearly, and remembered the promise I'd made to Pa shortly before he died to always watch out for her.

"Her new husband Andy's a good 'ne," he'd said to me. "And Ah'm proud to take him fer a son-'n-law. Ah expect he'll make your sister Judy right happy. Even so, you never can tell about things in life. Men come and go, sometimes even the good ones, and of course people die. But remember, son, you only got one sister. So Ah'm askin' you to promise me one thing. Anything happens that she needs help, you come a runnin'. Ya hear me, boy?"

"I hear ya, Pa. You know I will." I had replied, and I meant it.

Judy's letter started off all right with the usual—*Hopin' you're in good health.*—and—*Why aren't you settled down and married yet?*—nonsense, but then it turned serious. Seems Andy had taken a nasty spill trying to break one of the new bronc's he'd bought. Busted up his hip pretty bad. Doc Greene expected him to eventually recover, but he was going to be laid up for quite a spell.

Unfortunately Andy had borrowed against the ranch in order to bring in some new bloodlines. He'd been hoping to saddle break and then

18

sell enough riding stock to cover the mortgage payments to the local Savings and Trust. Now that he was out of action, the bank was calling in their loan.

I guess if I'd kept better in touch, I might have warned him about that bank. The manager was notorious for being a skinflint, and for years I remember my uncle Jake and Pa arguing about the S&T's strict loan policies.

"Never borrow against the ranch!" they'd warn.

"Too risky, especially with *that* outfit in charge," Uncle Jake would say angrily.

"Rather sell my soul to the devil than do business with the Savings and Trust," Pa would add, usually while lighting his pipe.

"It's the same thing as far as Ah'm concerned," Uncle Jake would reply without cracking a smile.

Apparently now that Andy was down, the cost of hiring more help wouldn't allow for enough left-over cash to cover their monthly mortgage payments.

Judith wasn't asking for a hand-out. That just wasn't in her nature, but the message was loud and clear. She was desperate and needed my help.

I haven't exactly been flush all that many times in my life, but fortunately the last few months had been good ones. I was able to dig up enough gold to help get her and Andy out of debt and at the same time still have a little left over to stake me to a small herd or maybe a ranch somewhere.

So that's why after receiving Judy's letter, I headed straight for the nearest town large enough to have an assay office, bank, and telegraph. Hopefully Blue Lake Ridge would not only offer a place to bed down in comfort, but would also allow me to cash in my diggings, and then send a check back to my sister.

CHAPTER TWO

It was an hour or so after sundown when I finally pulled up in front of the local livery. It was a well-built, two-story affair. The loft had ample space for hay storage and two large hinged doors were ajar, revealing a long hallway with about a dozen box stalls and another dozen or so standing stalls. Another smaller sliding door off to one side was open and led into a fairly good-size tack room just beyond the entrance to the stable.

It was evident that whoever built this place knew a lot about livestock. The top edges of the stalls were covered in metal strips to prevent horses from cribbing the boards apart, and there were several pitchfork racks built into the walls, high and deep enough to keep them out of the way of the horses. All the nails were countersunk and there were no loose wires that I could see.

What puzzled me was that a place so obviously well planned and carefully built would be in such total disarray. Large cobwebs hung from the rafters and doorways, and manure was scattered everywhere. Flies are always part of life at a livery, but here they abounded. Not only that, but the place reeked of old urine soaked hay and the water buckets looked as though they hadn't been cleaned in months.

I rang a large copper bell that was hanging from a hook at the entrance and heard a door open at the back of the barn. A tall thin gent with a large white kerchief trailing out of the rear pocket of his dirty gray trousers came out of the back room and walked down the hallway. As he approached I felt a strange sense of foreboding.

Every now and then I get what some folks describe as a premonition, a sort of a sixth sense. My ma used to joke about me having a dark side, but Pa just racked it up to having some Injun in me. Seems one of his grandparents had been a Shawnee medicine man, and Injuns are supposed to be more in touch with their spirits. At least that's what Pa used to claim.

I can't really explain it any better, but one glance at this stable manager told me that something was wrong; something was somehow out of place. Maybe it was the way he walked down the whole length of stalls without once glancing at the horses. All the other livery men I'd ever met had a way of constantly checking on their stock. They'd whistle, talk to, cuss at, or pat a horse as they passed by. At very least they'd glance over at the cayuses under their care.

The manager of this livery however acted as if the place was deserted. It seemed as though he could have cared less. This fellow was trouble.

"Help you with something stranger?" he asked, pulling one of his suspenders up over his shoulder.

He was about thirty, lanky, and had a short cropped black moustache with a small pointed chin beard like the ones on billy goats. He looked like he never had learned what a bathtub was used for.

"You the owner here?" I asked.

"Am now that old man Richter dropped dead," he sneered.

I didn't know who this Richter fellow was but it stood to reason that what he forgot about livestock management during his lifetime this sorry state of a man had yet to learn.

"Need to bed my stallion down for a night or two," I explained reluctantly. "I'd like him curried and grained, if possible. Hot bran him once if you can."

"This ain't no damn' hotel," he replied rudely. "You want him fancied up; go get the currycomb on the rack over there. You can do it yourself. Hay's in the bin, oats and hard corn in the buckets yonder. And in case you don't recognize it, the water's in the trough. Two bits a night, plus extra fer the grain." He stared back at me with his hand on his hips waiting for a reply.

I don't know who put the burr under his saddle, but I was too tired to argue. Besides, as my Uncle Jake used to say: *When you talk to the rear end of an ass, he don't get educated and you're likely to get crapped on.*

"Any particular stall?" I asked.

"Try one that's empty," he replied snidely.

"You got a name?" I asked abruptly. My patience was rapidly wearing thin.

"Turner. Mike Turner. And that two bits is up front," he snapped.

It was the straw that broke the camel's back. I was dog-tired when I pulled in, but now I was aggravated as well. I decided to make damned sure Turner knew it.

"Fine," I replied, leaning forward just enough to make my point. At six foot three, it doesn't take much to intimidate someone. I dropped two bits in his hand but never took my eyes off his. "But get this. His stall gets mucked out regularly while he's here or you'll find out how unpleasant life can become. You hear me, Turner?" I poked a rather large index finger right into the soft point between his chest and shoulder where I knew it was sure to hurt.

He flinched hard and then just shrugged, but I could see by the change in his expression that he got the message.

I shoved right by him without further comment and left the stallion in the cleanest box stall I could find. Turner rubbed his shoulder, turned away and retreated back into his room. Meanwhile I removed the palomino's saddle and bridle and stored them in the tack room. After I left the barn, I started out down the street towards one of the hotels I had passed on my way into town.

After walking past a half a dozen storefronts, I stopped in front of a boarding house that looked presentable. I had to smile when I read the sign over the entrance. The SHUFFLE ON INN was a small combination boarding lodge and eatery with a distinctively feminine touch. There were ruffled curtains over the windows and the door had been painted white with green and pink flower patterns around the edges.

Were it not for its name and the We Welcome Boarders sign, I might have mistaken it for a sewing parlor, or, as much as I hate to admit it, a high-tone social club. I almost looked elsewhere, but the smell of hot oven-baked biscuits floating through the open window was overpowering. Besides, I was too tired to go marching all over town looking elsewhere for a decent bunk.

Once inside, I found the mood distinctly different from the dirt and mud of the street. It was invitingly warm and cozy, somewhat reminiscent of the smaller out of the way boarding houses of New Orleans. Another strong but definitely agreeable odor of freshly brewed hot coffee wafted its way into the lobby from a small dining room that was back a ways, just off to the left of the registry.

In the center of the lobby there was an over-size crystal chandelier that hung from the ceiling directly over a round velvet sofa. Someone must have gone to a lot of effort to transport that particular set of furniture all the way here. I removed my hat and dusted off my chaps on the entrance mat.

For a second or two I once again debated leaving to look for something a mite more suitable for someone like me. Two things changed my mind. One was the comment I overhead from the eatery. A deep husky male voice bellowed: "Damned iffen this ain't the best Brunswick stew Ah ever tasted." The other reason appeared suddenly from out of the dining room, wearing a green apron around her waist. And what a waist it was!

"Please come in, stranger. We gladly welcome all boarders," the young lady said politely.

Her voice was equally as pleasant as the rest of her. I guessed her to be about twenty years old, and she had long auburn hair. I swear her eyes were violet in color. She spoke softly with a trace of a Southern accent.

"Don't want to mess up such an elegant rug," I said, averting my rather obvious stare away from her and down to the rug in front of the registry counter. "You see, I've been on the trail for awhile. And I reckon I brought most of it in with me," I added with an embarrassed smile.

I'm not usually all that shy around women, but, after all that time spent digging sod with a bunch of bearded old men, I guess her beauty caught me off guard. She was truly a meal for hungry eyes.

"Don't be ridiculous!" she exclaimed with a smile. "All the folks that board here work for a living, and most had to travel quite a ways to get here, too. You just come on over here and sign in. Make yourself at home. We'll get you a nice room, and then maybe you'll stay long enough to try some of our food." She passed around behind the counter and opened the registry.

"If that grub tastes as good as it smells, you may have a hard time getting rid of me," I joked.

She laughed and tossed her head back, unconsciously flipping her long hair back over her shoulder. After months of being locked away in a miner's cabin, the gesture almost made me pass out. I'd definitely been away from town too long.

"Well, then, you'll be here a while, 'cause it is that good," she said proudly. "So, if you want to stay, just sign in here," she said, passing me the book. "If you please."

"All right, I think I will, Miss . . . ?"

"My name's Millie. It's short for Mildred," she explained. "But don't ever let me catch you calling me that," she said sternly.

I laughed and nodded in agreement. She had a natural way of making someone feel right at ease. "All right, I won't. I promise." Then: "You can't really be the manager here?"

"And why not, may I ask?" she replied, feigning anger.

"It's just that I've been in a lot of hotels,

boarding houses, and such, and never saw a women so young running things. Especially not one so pretty, if you don't mind my saying so."

It was a feeble attempt at flattery, but in all fairness I was just getting my second wind.

She looked me over carefully and then, seeming to ignoring the remark, replied: "My father and mother came here from Memphis. They intended to set up nearer to the gold fields, but, as soon as they took one look at this town, they fell in love with it and decided to stay. They originally built this place to be our home. Dad started out by setting up a newspaper. We did all right at first, but a year later my father was killed when a runaway buckboard hit him." She paused a moment and sighed. "Mother didn't know all that much about the newspaper business, but she did know how to cook and tend to a home, so she sold the paper and put the profits into turning this into the eatery and hostel that it is now. When she died last year, I was forced to take over."

"Sorry," I said sincerely. "I know what it's like to lose kin."

She nodded back at me and hesitated some before continuing. "Thank you, but I've been lucky. The town has grown steadily and folks here seem to like the way I run things."

Just then a large elderly heavy-set gentleman came out of the dining room, wiping his mouth with a handkerchief. "I heard that, and we sure do." His voice matched the one I'd heard earlier. He winked at me and exclaimed rather loudly: "She makes the best peach cobbler in three states if you ask me."

Millie blushed a little, and then turned to select a key from the pegboard behind the counter. "You go on now," she said to him. Turning back to me, she explained: "Mister Ellsworth now runs the town's newspaper, but even so it seems to me he's prone to exaggerate. Now here's your key. Room Eight . . . up the stairs to the first landing, fourth room on the left. Nice view of the lake."

Ellsworth took a black bowler hat off the rack that stood near the entrance, and then opened the door. Before leaving, he paused for a moment, turned and replied with a laugh: "Nonsense, who ever heard of a newspaperman exaggerating?"

We both laughed and Millie tossed him a kiss.

After he was gone, Millie explained: "He's the one who bought the paper from my mother. He was a good friend of my father's, and I suspect he was overly generous with the purchase price. He was very good to my mother while she was alive and still watches out for me, too. He can be a little over protective at times though."

"Maybe so, but he seems to be a good judge of food," I said, referring to his rather ample girth. "I guess I'll have to take him up on that advice. Peach cobbler, wasn't it?"

She laughed back. "Not tonight. The special is

29

Brunswick stew, cornbread, and apple pie."

I picked up the saddlebags and Henry rifle that I'd set down next to the counter. "Fine with me, but you better put on an extra pot. I haven't had a good fresh cooked meal in a long time," I said. "See you later, ma'am. Fourth room on the left?"

"That's correct, and it's Millie, not ma'am." She smiled again as she exited from behind the counter and returned to the dining room.

I half expected the room to be pink and frilly with a canopy bed and lots of lace, but it turned out to be rather simplistic. That was fine with me as long as the bed was firm and free of bugs, which it was. There was a sideboard with a full pitcher of water and a rose patterned wash pot, in addition to a large mirror on the wall. One look at the mirror convinced me it was just as well that there weren't a lot of frills in the room. I was dirtier than the trail I rode in on.

Before I went looking for the first bath in over two weeks, there was one thing I still needed to do. As much I liked the inn, I had serious doubts about the locks on their doors, and I wasn't about to leave a load of gold lying around for anyone with a hatpin and half a mind to rob the room. I'd learned long ago that while some hotels might be nice, a lot of folks ain't.

The water pitcher was recessed into the side-board, but when I lifted the pitcher up to see if there was any space underneath to hide my bags, there was just an open hole into the cabinet below. I looked underneath and behind the sideboard, but there too, came up empty. I turned back to the bed and lay down to study the layout of the room. It was then that I noticed a small wood patch on the ceiling where apparently a lamp had once hung. It occurred to me that when someone searches a room they seldom think of looking up. I wouldn't even have noticed the patched hole myself if I hadn't been lying down directly underneath it.

I had to stand on a chair to reach the ceiling and found that the panel had been nailed into place in order to cleverly cover the hole. Using the edge of my Bowie knife it was easy enough to loosen a nail or two and slide the panel back. There was more than enough room up in the ceiling to hide my saddlebags. I slid them in, replaced the panel, and tapped the nails back with the butt of my knife.

That little chore finished I threw a towel around my neck and headed out the room and down the hall toward the bath, anxious to try some Brunswick stew and apple pie as soon as I was presentable enough.

CHAPTER THREE

When I finally made it down to dinner, I was shy a heap of beard. I couldn't bring myself to lose the moustache, though. Ever since I grew it people had stopped calling me kid, so I figured it had become sort of a necessary evil. As I was coming down the hotel stairs I noticed a sheriff going through the inn's roster. He looked up from the desk and watched me enter the dining room. As I waited to be seated, I could overhear Millie talking to him behind my back.

"That's right . . . that's him. But he's new in town. I don't know anything else about him. He seems nice enough though."

I glanced back over my shoulder when the sheriff left the inn. At the time I just chalked his curiosity up to a careful lawman who was simply checking out all newcomers to his town.

Millie walked up to me, tapped me on the shoulder, and smiled. "No need to wait. You can go ahead on in and sit anywhere you like," she said.

"But then I'd miss out on the pleasure of walking to the table with you," I said politely, hat in hand. I was starting to warm up my social skills, poor as they were. The bath must have given me more confidence. Millie blushed and gave me a shove. "You men are all alike. Two minutes in town and you're after the first girl you see. Now go and sit down over there." She laughed and pointed to the nearest table.'

"I'd be after you even if you were the last one I saw," I replied.

"You're just saying that 'cause you want a bigger piece of pie," she said, giggling and handing me the menu.

My stomach growled and I had to consider the possibility that there might be an element of truth in that. "Maybe so," I replied, "but I think I'll start with the stew first. And biscuits, if you got any."

"Sure do . . . best in the state. Coming right up."

As she headed to the kitchen I tried to make up my mind if she was nicer to watch coming or going. Fortunately, given as how the dining room wasn't very crowded, I had several opportunities to chat with her. Millie seemed real down to earth and had a pleasant personality and good sense of humor. I have to admit I was getting real distracted, but I still hadn't forgotten the reason why I had come to Blue Lake in the first place.

"Millie," I asked, "where in town might a fellow get some ore weighed and exchanged for currency? Maybe some place where I could get a voucher sent to another bank back home?"

"Well, you certainly could do all that at our

bank," she answered. "It's down the street, about four blocks south and over one block to the left. But tomorrow's Saturday and they're closed over the week-end. Tonight starts our Founder's Day holiday festival, which lasts through Monday, so I'm afraid the bank won't reopen till Tuesday morning.

"Any place else?" I inquired.

"Well, there is an assay office up the street that's open till two in the afternoon on Saturdays. They can change your ore for you and give you a chit for the bank, but I don't think they can make any direct transfers out of town, or such. I'm not sure but I think only the bank can arrange that. Maybe you could send the assay chit out by government mail, if you trust their delivery, and if someone else will accept the voucher. Banks got their ways of protecting things a little better, I suppose, what with their guarantees and such."

"Thanks. I'm in a bit of a hurry, so I think I'll check out that assay office in the morning. It's up the street you say?"

"Go out the door and turn left for two blocks. It's across the street from the saloon."

"Thanks," I replied. "And they weren't exaggerating about the food here."

"I figured you liked it. Folks who don't usually won't eat six biscuits and three bowls of stew."

I looked up at her a little sheepishly. "Didn't know you were counting. Been on the trail a while and I guess I got tired of camp cooking. Not that I wouldn't like your food any time."

"Big men need their nourishment," she said reassuringly. "Got any room for pie after all that?" she asked.

"Thought you'd never ask," I replied with my best smile. The pie turned out to be stolen from them Greek gods my ma used to read me about, and later that night I went to bed and slept like a bear in winter.

The next morning I considered my options. The saddlebags with my gold were still stashed in the ceiling hideaway and would be safe for the time being. I could leave them there over the weekend and wait for the bank to open, or I could check out the assay office and maybe get a jump on things. Never being much the slow patient type I decided on the local assayer, but, before I left the room, I separated out one small pouch and left the rest stashed back in the ceiling. No sense putting all my eggs in one basket. I didn't know this town and I didn't know who I could trust. If everything checked out and there were no problems I could always come back for the other bags. If not, I would simply leave the gold put until the bank reopened on Tuesday.

I went downstairs and tracked down a cup of coffee before going out. Millie wasn't around, which was a little disappointing, but the coffee was fresh, hot, and plentiful. The sign said help yourself, and there was a stack of doughnuts next to the pot, so I grabbed a couple. The first one practically melted in my mouth. I had to hand it to Millie—she ran a real first-rate place.

Finishing another doughnut, I chuckled to myself as I remembered my old friend Johnny. I had ridden the Pony Express for about six months during which time my pal Johnny Fry had rapidly become one of the more popular of the express men, especially with the ladies. Personally I couldn't figure out what they saw in him, but, whenever Johnny rode through a town or past a farm, it always seemed that his route was lined with young girls throwing flowers or holding out platters of cakes and cookies for him. It was Johnny, in fact, who once boasted that he was personally responsible for the invention of the doughnut.

According to Johnny's story, one of his female admirers wanted to get a jump on the competition, but, knowing that the Pony Express never stops for anyone, she went and invented the doughnut. That way, whenever Johnny rode by her house, all he had to do was stick out his finger and spear her doughnuts, right through the hole. By the time I'd left the Pony the story had become legend, but I never did find out if her invention allowed her to catch her man. Knowing Johnny, I doubted it very much. So, with a powdered sinker half hanging out my mouth and another in my hand, I headed out of the inn and down the street toward the assayer's. Millie's directions weren't hard to follow.

By day the town of Blue Lake Ridge wasn't half bad-looking. Of course, after all the time I'd spent in a mining cabin, the hustle and bustle of a town was a refreshing change. I've found that each town has its own unique sounds, colors, and smells. This one was growing, young, and energetic. To uppity big city folks Blue Lake Ridge, with a population of only six hundred, must have looked like a puny little burg with its mud pathways lining the drab and flimsy wooden buildings, but I didn't agree. As I walked down the street, I noticed a distinct energy to the place.

I passed a women's millinery store that carried such things as dresses, hankies, umbrellas, corsets, and such. There was new construction going on, too. The Blue Lake Ridge Surveyor's Office was enlarging, and had started adding on a lawyer's office. The Eureka Brand farm store had the latest in boots and saddles and there was a sign in the window advertising a free sharpening service for tools. Such things spelled optimism to me and a desire for more growth.

Continuing down the street, I passed the beginnings of a paper goods store with a sign that read Linkh's Printers. I was forced to smile when I noticed that their printing press had been set up even before the front door had been hung. Got to get the product out first I suppose. Early bird catches the worm and all that. Making the turn where Millie had indicated, I could see a large windmill set up to help tank water. It was located next to the town blacksmith. I also spotted the assayer's office up ahead, but as I passed the Brewster Brothers' Firearms and Cutlery Store, I just had to stop in. Their sign offered Firearms and Fine Cutlery, New and Used. Items Bought, Sold and Traded. While I did need to restock some minor items like percussion caps and cleaning oil, the truth is I couldn't resist checking out their array of weaponry.

I wandered around the store for a while, admiring their collection of razors and old powder horns. I took a Remington Rolling Block off the rack and noticed that it had been modified by adding different sights and shortening the stock some. I didn't like the change much and figured it had been made to fit a young boy or perhaps had been cut down for some rancher's wife. After collecting the supplies I needed, I headed to the front counter. While I waited behind a tall farmer and his son, I noticed an old pepperbox pistol in an open-top glass cabinet and picked it up, examining it with some interest. I always found the multi-barreled firearms among the most appealing. After the pair ahead of me finished, the salesman introduced himself.

"Hate to get a load of that in my gut," he joked, pointing to the pepperbox.

I shook my head. "Don't think I'd cotton much to it, either."

"Name's Rowland, may I help you? If you're interested in that piece I can get you a good price. We just took it in on trade."

"No thanks. Just looking and learning," I replied pushing my stuff over to him. "I'll take these items and some Thirty-Nine-caliber balls, if you've got them." His eyes followed me as I reached into my back pocket to take out my money. That's when he noticed my Navy Colt. Even for someone who wasn't in the firearms business, its scrolled inlays over the nickel plating and the pearl grips made it hard to miss.

"That's a Thirty-Six Navy ain't it?"

"That's right," I replied, "but the Thirty-Nines fit the bore tighter. In the right hands they add a little more accuracy," I explained.

"Well, I reckon if I had a nice pistol like that I wouldn't need this other one, either," he said, whistling in appreciation. "Want to trade it in?"

"Not a chance. Was a present from my grandfather."

"Quite a present," he remarked. "Must be a good man."

"He was," I replied seriously.

"Oh. I can see then why you wouldn't want to part with it," he said, totaling the bill. "But if you ever do change your mind, you'll be sure to give me first crack at it, won't you?" He put the supplies I'd purchased in a small paper bag.

"You might be a little long in the tooth by then," I replied, putting the bag in the leather shoulder pouch I always carried. "But I'll keep it in mind. Thanks for the supplies."

"You're welcome." Rowland nodded back at me. "Come again soon."

CHAPTER FOUR

I'd slept late that morning so I didn't quite make it to the assay office till about 11 a.m. There was already a line of men waiting impatiently by the time I got there. I've always been a little fidgety when forced into lines, especially when indoors, so while I waited for the assayer to finish with his other clients, I got bored and started fiddling with the scale weights he had left lying on the table. I tossed one in the air and caught it a couple of times before something struck me as odd. According to its markings, give or take a little, that weight should have weighed almost exactly the same as my Colt. I knew this odd little fact because a year or two earlier I had been hanging around a stockyard in Chicago and, on a bet, guessed the weight of a friend's pistol. I lost the bet and that led me to weigh mine for comparison. That's how come I knew exactly what it weighed.

After all the years of cleaning, handling, tossing, spinning, and drawing that Navy Colt of mine I knew exactly how it felt whenever I gripped it. When I tossed up and caught that assayer's weight it felt all wrong. It was much too light.

Puzzled, I rolled it around in my hand and

took a closer look. It had been cleverly done, but the weight had been shaved and repainted. I could feel the irregularities around the edge and the paint flaked off much too easily. I didn't say anything at the time, but, when the assayer gestured me to the weighing table, I quickly drew my revolver and set it down on the table.

"What's this?" he cried, shoving his chair back away from me. "I warn you, if you're thinking of making trouble, these guards will stop you faster than you can blink."

"No trouble I assure you. It's just that I'd like my gold weighed against that, rather than against your weights. See, I prefer an accurate count when it comes to my own gold. You needn't worry, though, I'm not out to cheat anyone. In fact, I have a signed certificate attesting to its exact weight from a certified Chicago scale maker."

The assay officer looked a little uncomfortable. "Nothing wrong with government weights. They'll do just fine." He pulled a small rag from his vest pocket and wiped his brow nervously.

"Maybe the government's might, but yours have been shaved," I replied angrily.

"What? What's that you say?" asked a burly bearded prospector off to my left.

"You makin' trouble fella?" one of the guards asked, stepping forward.

"Not me," I replied, shaking my head. "Never

was one to argue with a sawed-off." Oh, sure, there was a chance the guards weren't on the take, but then again maybe hell had already frozen over.

"Good," the guard grunted. He nodded to the pistol. "Nice and easy, then."

I gingerly picked up my Colt off the table with two fingers and dropped it back into its holster. "It's just that I couldn't help notice that the letter A is missing part of its leg on the USA mark on this weight and it feels light," I said. I guess I never really could resist pushing a point.

"Let me see that!" the black-bearded prospector yelled, grabbing the weight off the table. "Hey, he's right. Look at this," he said, passing the weight around to the others in the room.

"Give that back now!" yelled the assayer. "It's government property, ya hear?"

"They're all a bunch of cheats!" shouted one of the other men in the room, and, before I knew it, the whole place exploded with flying chairs, punches, and kicks. I knew it had gotten rowdy when bodies began sailing out the windows. Or should I say through them.

I ducked under a guard's punch and responded in kind with an elbow to his ribs. Off to my left someone broke a chair over another's head and two of the guards rushed at me. I tipped a table under one and he went sprawling. The other caught me in a tackle and we spilled out the door.

Once out in the street I managed to toss the man off me and quickly got back on my feet. Someone tried to shove his rifle in my gut, but I managed to deflect it upward and, by turning to my left, was able to flip him over in a hip throw. I wrenched the rifle from his grip and reversed the barrel, pointing it down at his face. That was when I felt a pressure on the back of my head and heard the very distinctive sound of a pistol hammer being cocked back.

"Freeze right there, cowboy, or it'll be the last thing you ever do. This is the law speakin'." I couldn't tell if that last part made me feel better or not, but the second push of the pistol barrel against the back of my head quickly convinced me to drop the rifle. I slowly straightened up and then turned around with my hands raised. I was relieved to see that the tall mustached gent facing me with the hog-leg in his hand did in fact have a star on his vest.

"Always was one to co-operate with the law," I said matter-of-factly.

"That so? Then you won't mind telling me what set off this Donnybrook?"

The assayer stumbled forward. His spectacles had one lens broken and he was bleeding from his nose. "Not what set it off, Sheriff. But *who!*" he exclaimed.

"How's that?" the sheriff asked, puzzled.

"This big galoot accused me of cheating, and

44

then started the fight. I want to press charges," he whined.

Fortunately I saw one of those weights lying on the ground near the doorstep. I walked over, picked it up, and flipped it over to the marshal. "See for yourself. It's been shaved. And to be more accurate, those guards threw the first punch."

"*Hmm.*" The sheriff tossed the weight up and down in his hand and looked it over. "Might be off, and then again it might not be," he replied, considering his options.

"Sure as hell is crooked," one of the prospectors added, rubbing his bleeding knuckles. "I checked it out myself."

Turning back to me, the sheriff holstered his pistol. "Well, I ain't no expert, but, seein' as how you got so many on your side, I guess we'll just have to shut this place down until further notice." Turning to the assayer, he said: "You come with me and I'll take down your side of it. I already know where he stands," he said, staring directly at me. "And see to it that you stay out of any more trouble while you're in town," he added, pointing a finger at me. "Until further notice this office is closed!" he yelled to the crowd. "You'll have to see the bank officer on Tuesday, after the bank reopens, about any exchanges. Now break it up."

I stood there watching the marshal leave with

the assayer in tow when someone slapped me hard on the back. I had the breath knocked out of me and thought for a second the fight had resumed until I heard the laughter. Turning around, I recognized the prospector with the black beard.

"I owe you one, lad," he said loudly. "Those cheats would have taken me for sure if you hadn't pointed out the problem with that weight. My pals and I dug hard for what's ours and we ain't gonna let no pipsqueak rob us blind. Besides, it was a good fight! So what do you say? Let me buy you lunch, eh?"

"Never was one to turn down a free meal," I replied, nodding. "You got a name?"

He stuck out his hand. "Turnbull, Martin Turnbull. Most folks call me Bull."

I could see why. My hand almost disappeared in his.

"William Grayson. You can call me Will, friend. So, you got any particular place in mind?" I asked after I finished dusting myself off.

He pointed a place out with his finger. "Right down the street a couple of blocks. Ain't elegant but they say the food's good."

"Sounds all right to me. Lead on, scout," I quipped.

We ended up in an open *cantina*-style restaurant. It had a long umbrella-like covering held up by four tall poles. One of the poles had a plaque that read:

Want to smoke? Go ahead, bub.
And it's okay to drop the ash.
But if you want to taste our grub,
You better be ready to show us your cash.

There were half dozen long wooden picnic type benches under cover and in the back was an open cooking pit and a couple of large stoves. A small sign pegged into the ground on a stake read: Today's special, Cooked Rabbit, Potatoes, and Bread—35¢. All the Chili you can eat—25¢.

"What are you having, Bull?" I asked. "The chili or the rabbit?"

"Hell, why choose? Let's have them both," he replied, laughing.

By the look of him, finishing such a meal wouldn't be a problem. 'Course then again I wasn't what you'd call petite, either.

The food wasn't half bad and Bull turned out to have a fair sense of humor.

"So what's your story?" I asked.

"My story?" He looked a mite puzzled.

"Sure, everyone's got one. Running away from a nagging wife . . . searching high adventure in distant lands . . . ," I explained.

"Oh, yeah, I got you," he replied. "Well, I guess you could say I was tired of getting hit on my thumb."

I laughed at him. "All right, but you're gonna have to explain that one."

"Well, it's like this. I come from a long line of carpenters. My father is a carpenter, his father was a carpenter as was his father before him. Hell I was born with sawdust in my blood. Got so much of it over the years, it's likely, when I die and shrivel away, they'll find two-by-fours instead of bones."

"Yeah, but it's usually good solid work, and most carpenters I've met seem to make a fair living," I noted.

"Sure, it is . . . if they're good at it. Problem is my ol' man didn't inherit the knack for it, I guess."

"What's that got to do with your thumb?" I asked, puzzled.

"Getting to it," he replied, using his sleeve to wipe chili sauce off his chin. "See, when I was a kid, my mother always used to insist on me helping my pa with his work. I didn't really mind learning the trade, but every time I went to him and offered to help, Pa always replied that he preferred doing such things himself. He told me if I really wanted to help, I could do so by holding the nails for him."

"Thus the thumb," I said, catching on.

"Right." He nodded. "Sure as shooting, every time that hammer came down my thumb was under it. Instead of learning to work wood, all I was doing was learning to flinch. Had to leave home in order to keep my limbs intact."

"Sounds painful," I admitted.

"It were that," Bull said, chuckling. "Wasn't till a year ago this traveling eye doctor came through town and found out my father needed spectacles. Must have done the trick 'cause last time Ma wrote me, she said Pa was getting a lot more orders for his furniture now that the drawers don't stick and the legs are all even."

"Well, that's a good thing at least," I offered.

"It is that," he nodded. "A little late to do me any good, though. I left some time ago after hitching up with a couple of friends from back home. We all came out here together when we heard rumors of gold strikes in the area," he explained. "Bunch of first timers, but we had ourselves some beginners luck 'cause we dug up a whole bunch of glitter."

"And that led you to the assayer's office," I noted.

"Where you may have just saved our bacon. And now you know the whole story," he replied, slapping me on the back.

I would have sprung for drinks afterward, in spite of the likelihood that Turnbull would have emptied a keg all by himself, but he excused himself and then headed off to meet one of the partners from his dig. I decided to tap into a keg myself and soon left in search of liquid refreshment.

CHAPTER FIVE

When I was about halfway down the street, the noon stage showed up. Its arrival helped break up the afternoon monotony as well as the crowd of men milling around when it nearly ran over half of them, myself included. I jumped back, barely getting out of the way, and gave the driver a dirty look. I left it at that, though, because I knew from experience how hard it is to handle a coach when it's hitched to that many horses.

Two years back I had driven wagons for Russell and Majors, hauling freight out of Denver to the camps. The wagons varied in size and weren't anywhere near as fancy as a Concord coach like this one, but the weight was about the same, coming in around one ton. A well-made Concord probably cost well over $1,200 and sat nine people inside, and several more on the roof if need be. It was a sturdy design with two thorough braces in its suspension and three inch leather shock absorbers. Some folks referred to them as "cradles on wheels." The mud wagons I drove weren't near as nice. They were as far from fancy as you can get. Those wagons were built for bulk weight, not comfort, and when hitched to a six-up of half-broke cold bloods things some-times got a little hairy, like the time Eddie Keetley took ill and asked me to fill in for him on one of his runs.

It was to be a boring three-week haul of supplies out to the mines, but I was glad to take over since the money was good and I had nothing else going on at the time. Eddie didn't really get a chance to fill me in on the contents of the wagon, and the voucher just said they were prepaid supplies. I assumed the load was made up of food and other sundries because the back was filled mostly with unmarked barrels and small wooden boxes like the ones food comes in. Anything dangerous like nitro or fragile like glass would have been well labeled. Also the station manager had mentioned that speed was of the essence, which also made me believe that I was freighting food that might spoil and other necessities earmarked for the miners.

Things were rather uneventful on the trip until I reached the Camp at Dry Gulch Falls. I had driven for three weeks without so much as a hiccup, but just as we pulled into the main street of camp, a cat bolted out of one of the tents chased by a large and rather mangy dog. Naturally, true to Murphy's Law, they had to run right under the lead horses, who immediately spooked and took off at a dead run. My arms were stretched so tight I feared I'd have to wear a longer sleeve length for the rest of my life. I suddenly found that my heart was having a hard time pumping while sitting up there in my mouth.

The wagon flew through the camp, which luckily consisted of one long straight road that was lined by assorted tents. It was long and straight that is until it reached the hardware store, at which point it made an almost ninety degree turn to the left. Why the hell they couldn't have built a nice gradually sloping turn is beyond me, but it's also beside the point. As I saw it, I had two options: run the whole rig straight into the only solid wooden structure in town and die a sudden and premature death, or try to take the turn, swerve the wagon, and die a sudden and premature death.

I decided to swerve. Sure enough the wagon flipped, as I had figured it would, and the hitch broke. I decided I didn't want to die crushed under a load of flour, after all, so I jumped. The question was whether to jump left or right off the wagon. Since I didn't really have any time to think all this through, I just leaped forward onto the last horse. It was more a reflex than anything else. While I was struggling to keep from falling or being trampled to death, I did manage to glance back in time to see the wagon make a full turn in the air before disintegrating in front of the store. It was a good half a mile before I was finally able to collect the reins—and my wits— and stop the team.

I considered not going back to camp since

the food had either all been spilled or spoiled and the millers were sure to string me up, but I had no choice. I had nowhere else to go and the horses needed watering. As the crowd gathered I thought about begging for mercy based on the ignorance of the young and the random nature of dumb animals. But much to my surprise, when I returned to camp, the men were all applauding. Seems the barrels weren't filled with flour, sugar, and molasses as I'd figured, nor did the boxes contain perishables. The whole wagon had been filled with boxes and barrels of nails, screws, bolts, staples, barbed wire, and hammers. By a stroke of luck I'd dumped the whole load right in front of the hardware store and for the most part saved the men the task of toting everything over from the freight office.

For two days I was the local hero and was made to feel right fine about things until I finally got back to Denver and Mr. Russell billed me for the lost wagon. It took me six months to work off the fine. It could have been worse except for the fact that I'd managed to save the team, and the miners in town had written me a letter of commendation.

Today here in town, although the driver had almost run me down, along with a third of the population of Blue Lake Ridge, I chuckled at the thought that at least he didn't flip the coach. I stopped to watch the passengers get out.

The first two folks off the stage looked like the usual types found traveling on any Western stagecoach. There was a rather fat gent with a derby hat and a carry bag. I figured him for a whiskey vendor, and the other man was probably a rancher on the way home from a sale.

The next one out the door was a reverend of sorts. He wore an oversize flat-brimmed brown hat and a long coat that was buttoned over his white shirt all the way up to his string tie. I thought the heavy leather-bound Bible in his hand was a dead giveaway as it was three times the size of any of the pocket versions I'd seen cowboys carry on the trail. It even had one of those fancy gold clips sewn to its cover to help keep it closed, protecting the pages I presumed.

Back home my ma used to drag me by the ear to Sunday meetings when I was young, but I'll admit that I never had much time for churchgoing once I'd left home. Even so, I'd be a fool to get on the wrong side of the Lord if I could avoid it, so, when the reverend reached for his suitcase, I walked over and helped him drag it down off the top of the stage. I had the height on him so it was easier for me to reach. I've always had a good set of shoulders, but his case was so heavy it practically pulled me over when I hauled it off the roof of the stage.

I was straightening back up when the stage door opened again. I looked up just as a lady was stepping out. Maybe merely saying lady doesn't do her justice. She was much more, what cowpokes describe as being "all woman." You could see it in her eyes. They were bright blue and daunting. Even hidden under the black shawl and bulky dress that she wore you could tell she had a quite an impressive figure. I remember a friend back home once who, after studying a picture of the famous actress Ada Menkin, startled me by suddenly proclaiming that her lips were in the wrong place. When I asked why, he pointed to his own mouth and boldly announced that they really belonged there, right next to his. That's the kind of effect *this* lady had on me.

I straightened up and stuck out my hand to help her down. She thanked me, and then turned to the driver and asked for her bags. I wasn't about to let an opportunity like that pass me by but— "Might I carry those for you, ma'am?"—was all I could think to say.

"Why, thank you," she replied looking me over for a moment. "But before I seek out a room, is there perhaps some place close where I might get a refreshment? It's been a dreadfully hot and dusty ride." She paused to brush some tiny speck of dirt off her skirt. I couldn't help but think that the gesture was exceedingly feminine in its execution.

I tried hard to maintain my composure. "Well,

ma'am, I'm new to town as well, but the Empire Room seems to be the nearest place," I answered, pointing to a saloon across the street.

"Is it suitable for ladies?" she asked, noticing the large Zang's beer sign above the door.

Suitable was an interesting word. In the Southwest there weren't all that many women around. Hell, in Texas you might not find a real lady for hundreds of square miles, except maybe for an Indian squaw or two. On the other hand, back east in the big cities, there were so many womenfolk they all had their own places to roost, such as ice cream parlors, tea rooms, and such. It seems to me Easterners divide their public places up into those for men only, those allowing saloon girls, and those for married folks or spinsters.

In these smaller middle-size Western towns, however, it isn't unusual to find a saloon or casino that caters to anyone who comes in, be they male or female, uptown folk or downtown types. There might be a section in the place for those interested in gambling, with someone dealing monte or perhaps a group playing keno, while in the same room another group of tables might have eats and refreshments for travelers. One thing they all have in common, though, is a long bar located somewhere in the room so folks can order a little hair o' the dog to take the edge off things.

"Rest assured, ma'am, no one will bother you in there or they shall answer to me," I answered boldly, and I will freely admit that I was playing it for all it was worth.

"How gallant you are," she said with a smile, taking my arm. "By the way, would you mind if the Reverend Fitzpatrick joined us?" She gestured for him to follow us. "He's such a nice man. We became well acquainted on the trip, and I'm sure he's as thirsty as I am."

"Of course I don't mind," I replied, lying through my teeth. After all isn't having a holy Joe along just what a man wants when he meets a pretty girl for the first time?

She turned to the reverend and smiled. "You will of course join us, won't you?"

The reverend nodded eagerly. "After that trip some liquid refreshment would be most enjoyable." He turned to me and offered his thanks. "Your kind invitation is most welcome, sir."

I rolled my eyes and, as much as I hate to admit it, actually grumbled. "Glad to have you along," I replied, fibbing once again.

"Then lead on, kind sir," she replied, looking up at me. I do believe I actually got a little weak in the knees just from gazing at her smile.

I would be willing to bet the pot that every eye was on me when we entered the saloon. Well, maybe not on me precisely, but certainly on us.

The Empire Room had a large main room and at the back was the long bar. To the right side of the bar was a stairway that led up to a row of six rooms on the second floor, running lengthwise over the bar. In one corner, off to the left, was a group of tables apparently set apart for newcomers, just off the stage. The right wall consisted of several gaming tables leading back to the stairwell.

I escorted the two of them to one of the tables on the left side of the room and stashed both their bags in a corner.

"I'll just get something to drink for you, ma'am," I said politely.

"A cold glass of tea would be nice," she said, taking a small fan from her handbag. "Mister . . . ?"

"Grayson, ma'am. William Grayson," I offered.

"If you don't mind, sir, I'll go with you," Reverend Fitzpatrick said, interrupting my train of thought.

"Sure. And feel free to stay at the bar if you want. No need to stand on formalities," I replied sarcastically.

"She is rather attractive, isn't she, my son?" he whispered as we approached the bar.

"Think so?" I asked.

He looked at me and broke out laughing. "And you don't?"

"Am I being that obvious?" I asked.

"I'd say you stand out about like an honest man in politics," he replied.

Sadly, when it came to women, I never could tell the difference between coming on strong and coming across as pushy. Maybe my size or young age had something to do with it, but it probably wasn't fair to take out things on the reverend, so I decided to back off and make amends.

"Barkeep, I'd like to buy my friend, the reverend here, a beer." I noticed the big Bible he was carrying under his arm and reconsidered my offer. I knew there were some religious types who didn't cotton much to the evils of drink. "That is," I amended, "if it is all right with you and the Good Book?"

"Nothing in my book against being sociable," he replied, lightly tapping his Bible.

"Good. At least that's settled. Barkeep, you got any cold tea?"

The bartender looked at the reverend and back at me and laughed. "Got the orders a little backwards, don't you?"

I didn't get it at first, but then it hit me. "No, it's not for me. I'll have a beer, too. The tea is for the lady over there." When I turned around to point out our female companion, I noticed some cowpokes from the bar heading in her direction.

"This don't look good," mumbled the bartender. The way they were walking made it apparent they were already several sheets to the wind, as my uncle Jake would have said.

CHAPTER SIX

I picked up the glass of tea, and the reverend and I returned to our table. Three cowboys were already standing near the woman as we approached. On second thought, surrounding her might be a better description. One was a tall thin sort with batwing chaps and a cross-draw rig. He wore a brown vest and a black flat-brim hat and had a small scar over his left eye. The shortest of the trio carried his pistol low on the right side, Texas-style. He also had an Arkansas toothpick on his belt and wore a dirty white ten gallon hat that had seen better days. The third man carried two guns forward, in crossed holsters, and wore an old cavalry campaign hat with a small feather in the band.

"Come on, honey, why don't we go on over to the hotel and you can entertain the three of us," the short one was asking, all the while leaning over her in the most vulgar fashion.

"I beg your pardon? What type of lady do you take me for?" she replied in disgust.

I looked over at the reverend who helplessly shrugged. The way I figured it, he probably wouldn't be much good in a real fight except to provide moral support, and that really wasn't the kind I needed right then. I shoved my way in, appearing to ignore the three men. "Sorry we took so long, ma'am, but we're back now," I said firmly.

"Hey, back up, stranger. This little filly is with us." It was the cowpoke with the big chaps who spoke.

"Now, gentlemen, I'm sure this can be settled peacefully," the reverend said peaceably. "Why don't I take you three over to the bar and buy you all a drink?"

Chaps acted first. "I don't think so." He made a grab for my shirt, but I simply tossed the ice tea in his face and head butted him into a nice sound sleep.

Shorty, who was facing the reverend, raised his hands. "You want some of this, Holy Man?" he asked threateningly.

The reverend shook his head vigorously and held up his Bible in defense. "I prefer to put my trust in the Good Book," he answered timidly.

"Well, you're getting some, anyway," the cowboy sneered.

Before I could help out, Shorty took a swing at him. The reverend ducked behind his Bible and the punch landed soundly on the book's cover. Shorty grabbed his hand in pain and looked up in surprise. The reverend was spun around with the blow and then stumbled back into his assailant. Luckily that big Bible caught the cowboy square on the chin and he fell backwards into the wall. He was clearly out for the count.

That left Feather Hat and me.

"Mister, I deal in lead," he growled angrily. "Go for your gun or I'll plug you where you stand."

It was my pa who taught me all about pistol craft and I remember his lessons well.

Assume every gun is loaded. Don't pick up a gun without checking it first. Never carry a gun unless you're willing to use it. Don't draw unless you mean to shoot and don't point or shoot unless you mean to destroy what you aim at. Any man who draws on you knows that someone will die. Just make sure it ain't you. It was all good advice and had served me well over the years.

Even so, I reckon I must have inherited some of Ma's more peaceful ways because I didn't automatically grab for my Colt. Instead, I took one last try at reasoning with him. Sadly experience has taught me that most times you can't reason with a mean drunk. This was another of those times.

"Mister, you sure you want to do this?" I asked. As soon as I opened my mouth, I knew it was the wrong way to play the hand. A drunk doesn't recognize the question as a peace offering or a way out, but, instead, takes it as a sign of weakness, one which he often misinterprets as fear. And that's just the way it happened.

"Don't try and back out of this," he snarled. "I ain't a-feared of no over-grown polecat. Just get ready to use that fancy shootin' iron o' yours," he continued, all the while squaring off at me and backing up a step.

I had to think fast or there'd be a killing that I wanted to avoid. After all, there was a fair chance the one getting killed might be me.

The man's hand drifted down to the butt of his revolver.

"You ever been to Tuscaloosa?" I asked suddenly.

"What? What the hell are you talking about?" he asked, puzzled at the strange timing of such a question.

"Right," I nodded. "Tuscaloosa. Ever been there?" I repeated.

"Naw. What of it?" he replied angrily.

"Well, seeing as how you're so all fired set on proving how tough you are, I thought you might want to prove it with a Tuscaloosa toe-off."

"A what? Toe-off? What's that?" He was even more confused.

"Takes real guts. You sure you want to know?" I goaded. "You think you're up to it?"

"I'll take you anyway you can think of. Just make it fast."

"A fella down in Tuscaloosa came up with it," I explained. "None of that old ten paces and draw crap. In a toe-off you stand right next to each other, boot pressed against boot. Toe to toe. Puts your draw right at the other fellow's chest." I pointed at him with my index finger. "No chance to run, duck, back up, or hide. You stand right there, hands up in the air, and at the count of three you drop 'em and draw. No way out," I said, sticking out my right foot. "So, you game or what?"

He looked down for a second before deciding. Meanwhile, I pulled the holster thong off my pistol hammer.

"Let's get on with it," he said finally, showing his right leg forward. He slid his boot right up alongside mine till they were touching.

My Colt was hanging loose in a Slim Jim holster that I had made to fit it by a leather smith in San Antonio. The holster was tied right down my leg. Nice thing about that particular holster was that, while the stitching went all the way around the sides, there was a small opening just under the pistol barrel to allow dirt and water to get out. Bullets, too.

"Barkeep," I said, "give us a three count."

The crowd in the bar gathered around, curious to see a real live Tuscaloosa toe-off.

"One!"

Positioned as we were, foot to foot, a fast draw would put a gun barrel right at the opponent's chest.

"Two!"

I could see beads of sweat on his forehead as he calculated the count. I did have to hand it to him. Even taking into account being drunk, there was no back up in him. I hated having to kill him.

"Three."

When you're standing that close, there's no time for hesitating, flinching, or slipping. You're either fast or you're dead. Fortunately for me when you don't actually have to draw, you tend to be a lot faster. In fact, by the time his hand started gripping his pistol butt, mine was already slip-pulling the hammer and trigger on my Colt. Truth is I wasn't at all concerned with pulling my gun free in order to fire. Positioned as we were, leg to leg, boot to boot, my holster was lined up directly over his foot. Instead of drawing I merely fired straight down though the bottom of my holster.

The ball hit his foot, shooting off a least two of his toes. The pain was so sudden and intense he dropped his gun and began hopping around the room, grabbing his boot and yelling: "You son-o'-a-bitch, you shot me in the foot!"

"Now you know why they call it a toe-off," I said, turning to the crowd. "But then again, better a toe than a lung."

The men in the bar just stared at me, dumb-founded. Then, from the back of the crowd someone started laughing, and after that it caught on with all the rest.

The sheriff came running in with a sawed-off in his grip. "I heard gunfire! What in the Sam Hill is going on here?" he asked.

"That fellow over there was takin' dancin' lessons," someone wisecracked from the crowd.

"The other two must have passed out from all the beauty and excitement of the ballet," another quipped.

There was more laughter all around.

Looking over at the cowpoke, who by now was flopping on the floor, screaming and holding his foot with blood-stained hands, the sheriff gestured to three men who were standing over at the bar. "Get this man and his friends out of here and over to the doc's office. Somebody clean this mess up. There'd better be a good explanation or someone's headed for the calaboose, and I mean *pronto*. So who's responsible for all this?" he demanded.

"I guess that'd be me," I replied, stepping up through the crowd.

"You again!" The sheriff shook his head angrily. "That's twice in one day and you just hit town. Like I said, this better be good."

"The gent on the floor was bothering the lady over there," I answered. "When I pointed out to him that it might be a good idea to reconsider his manners, he got a mite ornery and decided to push the issue. It was either him or me. Seems he lost a toe or two in the process."

67

"That so?" The lawman seemed to pause a moment to think things through. "Well, I suppose it's better to lose a toe than your life," he finally commented.

"I thought so, too," I replied.

"Hmm," the sheriff mumbled, all the while looking me over as if sizing up a side of beef. "You come with me." Taking me in tow, he then turned to the lady and approached her table.

"Sheriff Kent, miss. Name's Jeremy Kent." He removed his hat and bowed slightly. I had to hand it to him. He could be real smooth when he wanted to."

"June Elliott," she replied, fanning herself. "And its missus, not miss."

"My sincere apologies, Missus Elliott. I'm sorry you had to suffer this bit of unpleasantness, especially in my town. I must ask, however, does this man's story hold any water or is he just shining me on?"

"If you mean is he telling the truth about helping me with that ruffian, then the answer is yes. He did in fact come to my aid," she explained, lowering her fan. I couldn't help smiling at the sheriff. "Although," she continued, "it was in a rather violent way, if you ask me."

My smile quickly faded.

"For that happening while I am sheriff here I apologize once again," the lawman replied, giving me a dirty look. "Might I escort you back to your husband?" he asked her gently.

"I am a widow," she explained. "My husband died a short time ago, in a mining accident." She shook her head sadly. "I told him not to come out west, but he insisted. Then after I settled our affairs, I decided to return home to my folks. I was traveling on the stage that just arrived. I was hoping to go all the way, but it appears I may have to stay here a while. I'm running a little shorter on funds than I expected, and it's a long trip back home. I may actually have to find temporary employment here in town."

"I wish you luck, ma'am," the sheriff replied. "Anything I can do to help, just ask. Perhaps while you're here though, you might enjoy the town's holiday celebration this week-end. In fact, I'd be pleased to escort you, personally, in order to insure your safety. It would be in a purely protective capacity, of course."

"Why thank you, Sheriff," she replied, smiling widely. "I think I'd like that."

I felt badly for her recent tragedy, but, even though he wasn't such a bad-looking sort, I couldn't help noticing that for a recent widow she seemed to be sizing the sheriff up nice and quick.

Ruling out jealousy on my part over a pretty girl giving her attentions to another man, I still thought it seemed that the two were hitting it off a little too fast for my taste, especially given the seriousness of her loss. Then again I never really could read womenfolk all that well.

"In that case, might I ask you to accompany me to my office? You will be safer there. I can offer you a cup of coffee and you can help me fill out a report on all this. Of course I will see to it your bags are taken care of," he added.

I had to hand it to the lawman. It was as smooth an approach as I ever saw.

"Well, if you think I might be of service. Of course." Turning to me, Mrs. Elliott then smiled and extended her hand. "Thank you. I suppose I owe you my gratitude."

Before I could reply, the sheriff cut in: "Seems your story holds up all right, but see to it that you stay out of trouble from now on or the doc will have more than a foot to patch up." Sheriff Kent put his arm around Mrs. Elliott and escorted her from the saloon before I could even open my mouth.

"You're a pretty lucky fellow," someone remarked. "And I don't mean just the shooting."

"Huh?" I turned to see who had made the comment. It was the Reverend Fitzpatrick. "How so?" I asked.

"It's just that during my travels in search of the truth I've visited many a town like this one. I've found that most of the sheriffs I've met don't seem to cotton to newcomers stirring up trouble.

They usually come down quick on cowpokes, even if it ain't their fault. They often react very harshly. This one seemed rather lenient, if you ask me."

"That so?" I asked, though I knew it to be true.

"I suspect that if it wasn't for that rather attractive-looking lady, you'd have been run out of town on a rail. Maybe tarred and feathered to boot."

"Perhaps you're right, Reverend." I nodded my head. "So, can I buy you another drink to celebrate my good fortune?" I asked, changing the subject.

"I'd be most appreciative. This has been a rather disconcerting experience."

"You might say so, Reverend," I replied. "You might say so, indeed."

Turning to the barkeep, the reverend pointed to a small bottle. "We'll have two fingers of that."

I couldn't help notice that the bartender suddenly looked annoyed.

"What?" the reverend asked him. "Something wrong?"

"Would you deny a man of the cloth and his friend a harmless little shot of Who Shot Joe?" I added.

The barkeep just shrugged and poured the drinks.

"Why that bottle?" I whispered.

The reverend leaned closer. "Been watching

him for a while. Seems he serves everyone else from the larger bottles on the lower shelf. The only time I saw the bartender use that smaller bottle on the second shelf was to sneak a drink for himself. They all do you know. Anyway, I figured it must be the good stuff."

"Pretty observant," I noted with admiration. Raising my glass I toasted him and took a sip. "I like your style, sir."

The reverend swallowed, coughed a little, and added: "Amen . . . Amen to that."

CHAPTER SEVEN

After a couple more drinks, I bid an *adiós* to the reverend and went back to the inn. I figured a fist fight and a shoot-out constituted enough fun for one day and decided that a *siesta* before dinner might be better for my overall health. On the way up to my room, I couldn't help but notice a tall thin fellow leaning over the reception desk, talking to Millie. I didn't particularly like the smirk on his face, but Millie didn't give any indication that there was a problem. I overheard him saying something about meeting her later, and that sort of raised my hair a mite. I didn't know her well enough to be jealous, but I figured she could do better than this tall drink of water. I headed up the stairs, determined for once to mind my own business, but, in spite of myself, I still couldn't help glancing back down over my shoulder for a last look at the competition.

He had a dark complexion and his belt had a lot of fancy silver conchos on it that seemed a little out of place for these parts. It was just a quick glance, but the way he leaned so far forward over the desk and the smirk he wore was enough to convince me Millie could do a lot better with someone else. Someone like me, for instance. But then again as I've said, I never could read women too well and had learned a long time ago there's no accounting for taste.

I got to my room, unbuckled my holster, and hung it on the hook next to the door. My hat went on top of that, and then I settled down on top of the bed. I kicked off my boots and was asleep about the same time they hit the floor.

When I woke up it was a little past seven. I got out of bed and went to the vanity to splash some water on my face. When I looked in the mirror nothing appeared out of place except for a big bruise on my left cheek and a small scratch near my chin. There was also the beginnings of a bump on my forehead that I figured was the result of that head butt I'd given that cowboy. I washed the assorted nicks and scratches with the washrag that hung on the side of the vanity near the water pitcher and straightened my hair some.

They say that a Westerner undresses from the boots up, and then dresses from the top down. I guess I was no exception. Besides, my hat was close to my holster and I always felt a little naked without them on, especially when in a strange town. After my boots finally went back on, I once again double-checked the ceiling panel where my saddlebags were stashed. I was relieved to find that they were undisturbed. Noting a grumbling down in the general area under my belt, I opened the door and then headed down to dinner.

I was pleased to find Millie working in the

dining room without her concho-belted friend anywhere in sight. I stood at the entrance waiting to be seated. There was a good turn out and most of the room was filled. Millie finally came over and escorted me to one of the smaller round tables in the far corner. Out of habit, I chose to sit with my back to the wall and asked for a menu. I pushed the brim of my hat back and glanced up as Millie handed me the menu.

She took one look at me and gasped: "My goodness. What happened to your face?"

"You should see the other guy," I joked.

"Are you really all right?" she asked, concerned.

"Yes, fine . . . thank you." I'd hope to lighten the mood, but, when I saw the concern in her face, I quickly added: "Seriously, Millie, I hardly feel it. It's nothing, really, but thanks for asking."

"Do you mind telling me how it happened?" she asked, pulling up a seat.

I was flattered by the attention. "Had a little problem convincing the guards at the assay office that it was better for business not to cheat their clients," I answered. After looking into her eyes and considering the possibilities, I decided it best not to mention the second incident in the bar concerning the also beautiful Mrs. June Elliott. I figured what she didn't know wouldn't hurt either of us. Besides, when it comes to women I may be naive, but I'm not stupid.

"You in any trouble?" she asked.

"Nope. The sheriff just came by to say hello and introduce himself, but he left it at that. Seems there were others there with similar complaints against the establishment."

"I'm glad." She smiled. "I don't want anyone in town making problems for my guests."

"Forget it, it's fine. Can I entice you into having supper with me?" I asked hopefully.

"Love to, but I'm on duty as you can see," she answered, sweeping her arm around the room.

"How about an after dinner stroll, then? You could show me the town by night."

"Why, sir, you are persistent," she flirted back, feigning a thick Southern accent, "but I must decline. Sadly I have a prior engagement."

I remembered the fellow with the conchos and figured she meant him, but was smart enough not to let her see my disappointment. No sense in acting too desperate.

"Some other time then." I grinned.

"In the meantime, enjoy your dinner. Might I suggest the roast chicken?"

"Well, I'm usually a steak and potatoes sort of guy, but, if you suggest it, I'm sure it will be fine," I replied.

She stood up and smiled. "If you don't like it, the steak is on me."

After dinner I decided to walk off the meal. It was too bad I wasn't going to take that stroll with Millie, but the night was young, I had some money to my name, and in a growing town life is always full of possibilities.

While it's true that most of the cowboys and miners I've met over the years smoked like chimneys, I never quite got the knack of rolling a drag tight enough. Usually, when the wind blows, so blows my tobacco. I tried my hand at pipe smoking once, thinking it might make me look older and more sophisticated, but found to my dismay that there's a whole routine involved in it, what with preparing the bowl and constantly fiddling with the tobacco to keep it lit.

I guess pipes are more suited to slow careful folks who tend to think things over a little more than I do. Seems to me the whole pipe thing has more to do with getting rid of nervous tension than with any smoking pleasure. Besides, the different pipe tobaccos I tried tended to burn my tongue.

That doesn't mean I was adverse to a good cigar, however. Interestingly I had discovered long ago that the worse tobacco smells the better it tastes. There is nothing that beats a good cigar after a big meal for pure relaxation and enjoyment. The problem is finding a good enough cigar, because, sure as the sun will rise, a bad one will stampede a buffalo herd, not to mention eliminate any chance for female companionship.

Seems like most members of the opposite sex can smell a bad cigar from the next county.

Two things womenfolk definitely have developed since Adam met Eve is a sense of smell and a long term memory for recalling all the little mistakes men make when around them.

After leaving the hotel I happened to pass by a general store that had a box of stogies in the window. I was surprised to find they were still open, but, once inside, the shopkeeper explained that he usually worked until 9:00 in order to beat out the competition. When I asked him about the cigars in the window, he told me that they had just arrived the week before, from Florida.

"*El Dorados.* Had them shipped here all the way from Cuba. You won't find anything better, even in a fancy Denver social club," he proudly boasted. "Seventy-five cents each."

"Ouch," I grimaced. "For just one stogie?"

"Got me some five-cent ceegars, too, but you get what you pay for," he reminded me.

I was in a mood to splurge, so I bought one. I struck a Lucifer off my boot and ran the flame back and forth along the length of the cigar several times. Noticing my routine, the shop-keeper, a gent named Harry, inquired why I didn't just light right up and smoke.

"Why'd you run the flame along the length of the cigar like that?" he asked.

"Why sir," I answered, deadpan, "surely you

know a gentleman should always warm a lady before assaulting her."

"Ah, ha," he replied, smiling.

Before lighting the cigar and taking a puff, I also made sure to hold the match well below the tip. My uncle Jake once explained to me that running the flame that way warmed the cigar wrapper and allowed it to burn more uniformly. He also said that, if you put the match right into the cigar leaf, the sulphur smell from the match strike soaks into the cigar and ruins the taste of the smoke. I don't know if it was all true or not, but the ritual was fun, and the joke was always good for a laugh.

I tipped my hat and headed out the door. The evening air was refreshing, so after a half a block I stopped and leaned against a street post, enjoying the quiet evening breeze that was coming off the lake.

When you're out on a trail paying attention to small details can mean the difference between life and death. Even while relaxing, I had developed the habit of constantly looking around and listening for anything out of ordinary. Although it was safe in town, this was a personal habit I couldn't and wouldn't break. That's why I flinched a little when a man suddenly stepped out of the shadows across the street. I recognized him immediately as one of the customers eating at the inn. It wasn't hard as he was wearing a rather distinctive cowhide vest and his hat had a bright red band on it.

The cowboy didn't pay me the slightest attention as he walked by and made no threatening gestures of any kind, but I'm kind of suspicious by nature and don't like folks who walk in shadows. My right hand was down by my holster and I kept an eye on his back, relaxing only when he kept on walking down the street without even a glance back.

My eyes finally came to rest on another figure that could only belong to Mrs. June Elliott. I tossed the remains of my cigar on the ground and started toward her, following quietly behind the cowboy with the red hatband.

The man passed right by her, tipped his hat, and simply kept on walking. I settled down once he turned the corner and disappeared from sight. I pulled a tiny box of Sen-Sen licorice mints from my shoulder pouch and popped two pieces in my mouth. I'd bought them along with the cigar. They burn like the fires of hell on your tongue, but I learned a long time ago that fine ladies tend to avoid men with cigar breath.

I tried not to appear as eager as I felt, so I began whistling softly as I strolled casually down the street. The truth is I could smell her perfume in the air, and, as I said before, both the night and I were young and fresh.

CHAPTER EIGHT

"Mister Grayson, over here."

Mrs. Elliott stood alone in the street, around the corner from the livery stable, and was beckoning to me. Even from afar, one had to admit she was a striking figure of a woman.

"I'm sorry to trouble you at so late an hour, but would you mind very much escorting me on a simple errand?" she asked, once I arrived at her side. "It's a little late, and I'd rather not be alone in a strange town."

"Will . . . please, ma'am," I replied, sweeping my hat down in what I hoped was a most gentlemanly manner.

"Will it is then." The way she said my name made my chest squeeze. "Call me June," she added.

"I'd be glad to accompany you, a real pleasure, June, but, if you don't mind my saying, I sort of thought you might be escorted by the sheriff tonight."

"Well, I will admit he is most persistent, but it seems he's also presently tied up on a legal matter, and I have a small errand to run. Besides, after your impressive demonstration of physical skill in the bar earlier today, I do believe I will be safe with you at my side."

I almost blushed. "Most assuredly so," I responded earnestly. "So where are we headed?"

"The gentleman at the livery stable said he might have a horse and buggy I could use tomorrow, as long as I reserved it tonight and made sure to return it on time. He told me I should check back to see if it had become available. I know it is getting late, but would you mind terribly escorting me over to the stable, just for a moment?"

She smiled so nicely, it was impossible to refuse.

"Of course I will, although, if you ask me, I do believe you're being overly generous referring to that livery fellow as a gentleman," I said, straight-faced.

She covered her mouth to stifle a laugh. "I'll admit I was being somewhat polite. You sure you don't mind my imposition?"

"No, not at all. It'll give me a chance to check on my stallion. So why are you looking for a rig, Missus Elliott . . . excuse me . . . June? Planning on staying here for a while?"

"It's over this way, I believe," she said, pointing toward an alleyway.

I never did get an answer to my question. Frankly I've never been partial to crowded streets or narrow alleyways, and, under any other circumstance, I probably would have avoided the short cut. Shamefully I'm forced to admit that I was too absorbed in my rather attractive companion to pay much attention to a simple alleyway. True gentleman that I was, however, I did go in first in order to make sure it was safe. It's not that the alley was particularly ominous or poorly lit, but there were several large barrels and some old boxes strewn about that should have caused me to pause and reconsider. Unfortunately I didn't. Halfway down the alley, I turned to look back for her. Apparently someone must have been hiding behind one of the crates, because I felt a blow to the back of my head and suddenly everything started spinning and then went black.

I awoke sometime later. Exactly how much later, I have no way of knowing, except that it was much darker out. My hands were bound, and I was laid, face down and sideways, over my horse. I could tell we were heading uphill out of town. My head hurt almost as much as the time I was twelve and found my uncle Jake's still, unattended, with an old tin cup lying nearby, next to a new batch of moonshine.

Even tied down as it was, I could still recognize my own saddle, and I knew I was being carried by my palomino stallion. It was too dark out to get a good look at the men leading my horse, but every now and then the moon reflected off the lakebed below, and I could tell we were heading uphill, out of town.

Common sense told me that when someone

hits you from behind and ties you across a horse in the dead of night, they probably don't have your best interests in mind, so I decided to play opossum and just listen. There were three or four men out in front, but apparently no one behind me or off to the sides. I had awaken in the middle of an argument of sorts.

"God damn middle of the night," one of them cursed. "Why didn't we just shoot him in town, or say he died evading capture?"

I hoped they weren't discussing my immediate future.

"You still don't get it," another replied. "Look, you fool, go over it again one more time. If there's no body, it makes it look like he got away with it, instead of allowing for doubt and having anyone looking for us. That's why we got to hide the body where no one can find it."

I wondered what the "it" was that they were getting away with, but I had a pretty good notion whose body they were talking about.

"So that's why we got to lug this big galoot all the way out here?" the first one asked.

That remark gave me an even better idea who they were referring to. I tried to catch a glance at them, but from my upside down angle all I could see was a rather unusual Mexican-style rowel on the end of one of their spurs.

"Right. Same reason we couldn't shoot him in town," the one with the Mexican spur explained.

"Someone might have heard the shot and come a-runnin'. We can't have anyone know what's what. It's got to look like a clean getaway, remember? This way it's all nice and clean, real quiet-like. And if you didn't hit him hard enough in town, well, then, we'll just put one in his head once we're far enough out. Then we bury the body where it won't be found."

In spite of the Mexican spur I couldn't detect any noticeable accent.

"What about his horse. Mighty nice. Fact is I'd like him for myself," another commented.

"Maybe later, but remember we can't risk having him recognized, either. We'll keep the palomino hidden with the other mounts till later. You can talk to the boss about him when we leave. For now, let's just worry about dumping the body."

For some reason, I was getting a little offended at constantly being referred to as "the body." I decided not to express my displeasure, however, at least not out loud, and especially not right then and there. What I did do, instead, was try to find a way out of remaining "the body" and getting back to living my life, hopefully for a lot longer than these men had planned for me.

My wrists were bound too tightly for me to work them loose, but at least my feet were free. I couldn't reach anything on my saddle that under the circumstances would be of much use to me, and what with my horse being led by the reins, trying to take off at a run was out of the question. Besides, the way they had me thrown over the saddle sideways I wouldn't get very far without falling off. Falling off . . . That got me to thinking.

Even face down I could tell we were heading uphill and toward a bend in the trail. There wasn't much on my side of the trail except a steep drop off. The lake was very far below. Maybe too far, but, then again, I didn't have much of a choice. There was an open patch right where the trail curved that might work for what I had in mind. Slowly I used the stirrup leather to pull myself farther down the side of my horse. I hoped the saddle wouldn't creak or that they wouldn't notice me squirming. Fortunately the gang seemed unconcerned with "the body" and kept looking up the trail.

I tried to picture the road in my mind. It was narrow, only wide enough for two or three horses abreast. With a rock wall on one side, the lake on the other, and armed riders in front, it didn't look good.

Tied as I was, I couldn't ride the horse, but I sure as hell wasn't about to just roll over and die. Roll over and die. Maybe that's just what I would do. Roll over. There didn't seem to be anyone behind me. I thought about landing behind my horse and trying to roll away.

I knew I was almost as good as dead, but almost ain't the same thing as being all together dead. I never much liked others trying to run my life for me, and I sure as hell wasn't going to let someone else spell out my death. Even if I didn't make it, at least it would be my decision, not theirs. I'd decide as to how, what, where, and when. Better to go that way. Then again, I might just fool everyone and survive.

I managed to inch over the saddle, grabbing the stirrup leathers, just enough to the point of falling off, which was exactly why I was doing all that wiggling to begin with. Once we made the curve, I pulled one last time and threw my feet upwards toward my head. I hit the ground, hard, and one of the horses shied. I rolled once before hitting the edge, but unfortunately I couldn't stop rolling, and, before you could remember the Alamo, I was over the cliff.

Sometimes what seems like a good idea at the time turns out to be something entirely different. Of course all that didn't matter since as I fell through space there wasn't time to reconsider my choice. All I knew was that it was a long fall and much farther down to the bottom than I liked. I have made a few good dives in my life into rivers and creeks, but you'd hardly call what I was doing a dive. It was more like a terrifying spin head over heels down into the lake far below. It was a very long drop, and

I do believe I screamed the whole way down.

After tumbling for what seemed like forever, I hit something in the dark, probably a tree branch. It hooked my arm, snapped the rope around my arms, and snagged my left shoulder. I felt something pop and continued to plummet downward. As I said, it was a very long way down.

I don't really know what it sounded like in the world outside my head when I hit the lake, but I can tell you what it felt like to me. It hurt like hell. Thankfully I hit the water, feet first. It was more luck than anything else, but, even so, I still felt like my feet had been hammered straight up into my gut. I blacked out for a moment or two, and when I came to, I found myself being hauled down into the water by the weight of my boots, holster belt, and clothing. I kicked as hard as I could until I finally broke the surface. I gulped as much air as I could and began thrashing around. Although my feet hurt and I couldn't use my left arm much, I knew the pain meant I was still alive. How long I would remain that way I couldn't tell, but I was trying my best to make it as long as possible.

They say that there's always light at the end of a tunnel. While that may be true, I've found that occasionally the light's from an oncoming train. This was another one of those times. Just as I was managing to get control of my breathing and relax some, along came that locomotive. This one arrived in the form of a floating tree trunk. Imagine, a whole lake to float around in, and this thing has to slam into me at full bore, branches and all. It pushed me back under and seemed to take forever to pass over. When I popped back up, I was sure I had left one of my lungs down below on the lakebed.

The trunk spun and rolled around and I was pulled back into it, snagged by a long branch that was trailing behind. Just about the time I thought I'd bought the farm, I realized the situation might not be all bad. If I could manage to climb up on that trunk, or, at the very least, wedge myself into a branch above water level, I might be able to float to safety. The problem was, it was a very big trunk and my left shoulder was hurting so much I couldn't pull with it. While there were a lot of smaller branches, the tree itself was wet and slick, and I couldn't get a good grip. I was fading fast when I suddenly remembered my Bowie knife. I reached across with my right arm to the side of my belt where I had the sheath tied, and pulled the knife free. It had a fourteen-inch blade and was thick as an axe. With my last ounce of strength, I kicked upward and thrust forward, rising out of the water. As I fell downward, I sank the knife almost up to the hilt. I used the knife as an anchor to pull myself up and over, collapsing onto the top of that trunk. As I lay there, staring at the knife's Buffalo horn handle, my mind began to wander.

About three years back, a half dozen of us had been hired as scouts, guides, and hunters for the railroad. We had just entered buffalo territory, and since the crew was getting tired of prairie hens, rabbits and beans, Lew Daniels and I rode out ahead to find some real meat.

I never liked hunting for sport, or trophy, but I got nothing against hunting for food, especially when I'm one of those going hungry. I was a better shot than Lew, but he was a better tracker than I was and had more experience with buffalo herds. Lew had been a runaway slave and had spent time living among the Cheyennes. I never saw anybody better around livestock than Lew. Although they say there ain't no rider that can't be throwed, if there was an exception to the rule, I'm sure it was Lew, and I say that not being half bad on horseback myself.

After about a day and a half of riding, we came across a small herd, grazing out in the open. Lew suggested we approach on foot, so we ground tied our horses to a couple of heavy rocks and started from a point downwind of the herd. There was a clump of scrub bush that offered some cover, so I used it for my hunting stand while Lew continued to stalk up close. According to what Lew had taught me, if you shoot the head bull, the rest of the herd just stays put and doesn't panic.

At least that was common thought at the time.

This time things didn't work out quite as expected. At first, all went well. Lew got close enough without any problems and lay down on a knoll with his musket resting on a shooting stick he'd made out of a forked branch. The lead buffalo didn't pick up his scent, and the herd continued grazing quietly. Once Lew fired, however, something odd happened and things turned ugly, real quick. Two of the beasts grazing nearest him spooked and charged right at him. He was using a single-shot Sharps rifle and didn't have time to reload. The Henry rifle was faster. My first round caught the first buffalo between the eyes and brought him down stone cold. Lew turned and started to run, but knew it was no contest. He figured there was no way in hell he could outrun that beast. The second bull was closing fast when I hit him just behind the shoulder. It was an angle shot and must have been one of my more lucky ones, because something gave inside the bull and he collapsed about two feet from Lew's leg, gave a loud grunt, and rolled over. Lew turned back toward me, gave a combined look of shock and gratitude, and then promptly collapsed to the ground.

That night, sitting around the campfire, Lew was rather quiet and serious.

"Why so glum?" I asked, trying to cheer him up.

"To tell you the truth, Will, I never come that close to the Promised Land before. If it weren't for that lucky shot of yours, well, I just don't know," he replied, shrugging his shoulders.

"Luck had nothing to do with it, Lew," I lied. "I just didn't want you to have to walk too far when you went to skin him. Thought I'd deliver him real close-like."

He laughed, but then turned serious again. "You saved my life back there. I thought I'd bought it, for sure."

"Oh, come on, Lew, liven up, son. You look like something the cat dragged in. I've known you for what . . . going on a year and a half now . . . and I've seen you in tough spots before. You did all right."

"I know that. It's just that I never actually shook hands with Mister Death before. This time I saw his hand stretching right out for me."

"I'll admit it doesn't get much closer than that, but, then again, I'm still with you, so if you're still worried about it, don't be. I'll protect you."

Lew threw a stick at me and laughed. "Cut the clowning, will ya? I'm trying to tell you I won't forget what you done for me. Anything you need, just shout. I owe you one."

I shook my head and pushed my hat back on my head. "You don't owe me anything, but if you want to do something for me, toss me your knife for a second. I want to cut me a slice of meat. I lost mine on the trail a week ago," I explained.

We passed the rest of the evening chatting until my brain told my lids it was time to get some shut-eye. The next morning, there was a shiny Bowie knife, with a slick black buffalo horn handle, stuck in the ground in front of my face.

"What's this?" I asked.

"Looks like a knife to me," Lew replied, putting the coffee pot on the fire.

"I figured that much out for myself, but where'd it come from?" I asked.

"Had the blade for some time now. A blacksmith shaped it out of an old wagon spring for me. Was just looking for the right handle to come along for it. Guess I found one."

"Sure is a beauty." I tossed the knife from hand to hand. "Good balance. But why use a wagon spring?" I inquired.

"Came upon an old abandoned wagon a long time ago," he explained. "Every other piece of metal was all rusted and pitted, except for that spring. Still shone like it was brand new. It's hard as a rock, but holds a good edge. Just needed the right handle for it."

Rubbing my thumb along the knife to test its edge, I nodded back in agreement. "Very nice," I said. Holding it by the blade, I handed it back to him, handle first.

Shaking his head, he said: "Naw, you keep it. You need one."

I realized then that he must have been up all night carving a new grip out of buffalo horn. "I can't keep this, it's too much. Honestly, Lew, you don't owe me this. You'd have done the same for me."

He just glared at me. "Iffen you don't keep it, it'll just stay here."

Gratefully I looked down at that polished buffalo horn handle back then, just like I was staring at it, now, in the middle of Blue Lake.

Lying on that tree trunk, floating in the middle of that wet, cold lake, I began to pass out. The last thing I remember is gripping that black-handled knife for dear life and mumbling: "Thanks, Lew. I guess we're even now."

I don't know how long I hung there, but it seemed like an eternity. An old familiar voice in my head kept repeating over and over: *Hang on, keep going, you can make it.*

I must have been hallucinating. The voice sounded just as it did when I was ten. *Hang on, keep going, you can make it.* Another time, another lake. Pa always told me that swimming in a lake was different; he just never got around to explaining how. That particular pond back home wasn't anywhere near as big as Blue Lake was, but it had an island in the middle, and to a ten-year-old that meant buried pirate treasure and all sorts of adventure.

As a child back home, I had taken to swimming

94

right off and had spent lots of summer months with my friends, splashing around creeks and small ponds in the area. At ten, I felt I was good enough to swim the English Channel if need be, but, truth be told, swinging from a rope into a creek or splashing around the shore of a pond isn't the same as long-distance swimming in a fairly respectable lake.

Pa had taken me along on a short three-day trip to gather some supplies and to pick up a new buggy for the ranch. On the way back, we stopped along the shore of that lake. I took one look at the island in its middle and knew I had to swim out to it.

"Looks pretty far for a ten-year-old iffen you ask me," Pa cautioned.

"It'll be all right, Pa. I done swum lots farther," I fibbed.

He looked at me suspiciously and glanced over at the island. Pa then shrugged his shoulders. "All right, but be careful. While you're havin' fun, I'll just tend to the horses and make us some lunch."

If Ma had been along there wasn't any way I would have gotten away with it, but I sure wasn't going to point that out to Pa. Instead, I stripped down and jumped right in. I started swimming and knew that in a few minutes I'd be standing on unexplored island territory. I was young, strong, and in high spirits. After about ten minutes I stopped, treading water while looking forward at the island. For some unexplained reason, it didn't seem any closer. I took a deep breath and plowed forward. Nothing was going to deter me.

After another twenty minutes, I was beginning to get tired and couldn't understand why I wasn't already on shore. It hadn't looked that far away. Of course, at the time I didn't understand that the reflection of water on a lake often makes objects look closer than they really are. Another thing I overlooked was that this lake had some fairly good currents. I had aimed straight for the middle of that island, but the water current kept pulling me off course. I couldn't tell all that while in the water, but, from the shore, Pa was surprised and not a little upset at the way I was zigzagging my way to the center. I was swimming much harder and much farther than need be. I should have aimed up current and allowed the lake to pull me into the island. I know that now, but back then that one little missed detail almost killed me.

I began to use every trick I could think of to keep going. I floated on my back. I did the breaststroke for a while, and then switched to the side paddle. Finally the time came when I didn't have any more strength and couldn't swim another stroke. I lifted my head up and just floated as best I could. I was almost there, but found I couldn't move my arms any more. To this day I don't know why I lowered my legs, but boy was I shocked when they hit sand. I dropped to my knees and rose up. To my surprise the water was only up to my ankles. I had reached shore and hadn't known it. I guess it's true what they say about people being able to drown in just a tablespoon of water.

Where I got the strength I don't know, but I lunged ahead until was sitting on the beach of that island. Somehow the desire to explore had left me. The exotic tropical island suddenly looked more like a stinking mess of silt and tangled tree roots. Pa waved at me from camp and I waved back. That's when the realization hit me that I'd have to swim back. I groaned and rolled over in the sand to catch my breath.

I laid there for a minute or two, resting, but I knew that I'd have to leave right away. If I stayed there any longer, I was sure to cramp up, and then I wouldn't be able to swim. Even if Pa realized the danger I was in, it would take him a long time to swim out to me, and then he'd have to swim all the way back in the dark, dragging me alongside. There was no way I'd allow that to happen. I'd die of embarrassment. Better to risk the lake.

I got back up, took a deep breath, and dove into the water. I truthfully don't remember any of the swim back or how long it took, but I do remember a voice inside of me repeating over and over: *Hang on, keep going, you can make it.*

I did hang on, and finally Pa met me at the shore with a towel and a hot cup of coffee. I took two sips and curled up under a tree into one of the soundest sleeps I can recall.

Hang on, keep going, you can make it. This time I hung on to that tree trunk in the middle of Blue Lake, squeezing for dear life. Eventually I couldn't help myself and I finally passed out.

CHAPTER NINE

I woke up who knows how much later in what appeared to be a plank cot inside a log cabin of sorts. It was old and makeshift, but, seeing as how I was grateful still to be breathing, it seemed right cozy to me. I tried to sit up, but my side hurt so much I cried out in pain. I lay back down and took stock. Obviously I was still alive, the pain in my side and legs made that plain enough. It figured that, if someone had taken the trouble to carry me here and not kill me on the spot, I probably wasn't at any gang hide-out. Whoever that gang had been, they would still be somewhere back on the trail, and they would have killed me if they had been the ones to find me. I was just thankful they hadn't succeeded.

The cabin was empty except for a fat old yellow and white tabby cat lounging in the corner, who seemed to be content chewing on the remains of a field mouse. There was a red and white blanket nailed over the only window in the place, but it was pulled down so I couldn't see exactly where I was. The room was rather small, but there was another tiny area off to the right, probably used as a second sleeping quarter or perhaps a storage area. There was a thick round wooden table in the middle of the room and a fireplace behind it. The walls were covered with posters of old actresses and stage shows from years past. They looked strangely out of place. Scattered around both rooms were several trunks of different sizes. From the rust on the clasps and hinges along with the chips and cracks in the wood, they obviously had seen their fair share of travel.

My boots were on the floor next to me, and my shirt was off and hanging on a chair next to the bed. I still had on my pants, my belt and holster. My heart skipped a beat when I reached down and realized my holster was empty. My prize pistol was gone!

The door suddenly opened and an old man with long hair, a white beard, and a well-worn 'coonskin cap came in. I immediately noticed he was holding my Navy Colt. He must have seen my hand over my empty holster, because he spoke right up.

"No need to worry, son. I ain't a fixin' to use it. I ain't even planning on robbing you of it. Never was much good with a short arm. Hell's bells, I ain't even much use with a long rifle. That's why I always have that shotgun, over there, with me." He gestured to a side-by-side twin-hammered double-barreled leaning against the wall in the far corner of the cabin. "But this a pretty piece. I decided to clean it for you while you was out. Wouldn't want the barrel to rust after being in the water. Had to go out back to get some grease, though. Reloaded it fer you. You been up long?"

In my condition it was a lot to take in. I shook my head. "Nope, I just woke up. You fish me out of the water?"

He nodded and laughed. "Biggest thing I ever caught. Had a hell of a time getting you back here. Had to make a second trip to go get my burro."

"Don't know how to thank you," I replied as he handed the Colt back to me.

"No need. You'd a probably done the same for me."

"One thing's for sure, I will from now on . . . Mister?"

"Name's Kleiner. Albert Kleiner. Folks nowadays just call me Old Al. Mighty pretty piece," he said, watching me handle the Colt. "Don't believe I seen one quite like it."

I did a highwayman's roll and dropped the pistol into my holster. The Colt was nickel plated with elaborate scrollwork and had a set of real mother-of-pearl grips. Admittedly it was quite the work of art. Al watched me with interest.

"I know. I know," I said. "It's much too much for a plain old drifter like me, but it was a gift." I ran my hand across the pistol grip.

"Awful nice gift, if you ask me," he commented.

I nodded in agreement. "One of the last things I ever got from my grandfather. I couldn't part with it, no matter how hard things got. I had this holster stitched up for me in Texas, and, well, the rest is history, as they say."

"Got a feeling it's been an interesting history," he remarked, stroking his chin.

"So far, I guess it has," I answered truthfully.

"You in much pain?" he asked.

I proceeded to check myself out again. Admittedly there were a few more aches and pains than usual, but nothing seemed terribly out of line. My left shoulder and one leg were bandaged. "Roughed up some," I answered, "but I been worse off."

"Near as I can tell, you banged your side real good, although it don't look like any ribs are busted. Your left ankle is swoll' up a mite, but I think it's just a sprain. Leastwise it don't move funny. Big problem was your left shoulder. It was all out of socket, so I popped it back in. Got to keep it immobile a spell," he explained.

"You a doctor?" I asked.

"Oh, let's just say what with all the gravel I tasted over the years, I managed to pick up a few things. A doctor, me? Heavens no. Just the opposite. Son, you are looking at one of the finest thespians that ever trod a stage."

"Trod a what? What's a thespian?" I asked confused. My head was still spinning some.

"Actor, my boy. Actor. Why, in my day I was one of the best. Started out as a kid in Illinois, but, before I was finished, I'd worked my way up to playing Colonel Nimrod Wildfire in James Kirke Paulding's *Lion of the West*. Folks raved at my performance in Washington, New York, and Richmond. I wasn't the first, but I was much better than that ham James Hackett, even if I have to say so myself."

"Which you just did," I pointed out. "That where you picked up that 'coon-skin cap?" I asked.

He raised his eyes and removed the hat. "A little remembrance of better times, I guess."

In my experience, that usually meant either liquor or some woman, but, seeing as how this kind old man had just saved my life, I wasn't about to pry.

"How long have I been here?" I asked.

"Two nights and today. Judging by that knot on your head, you took a pretty good wallop during the fall."

"Got that before I ended up swimming with the fish," I replied, feeling the back of my head.

"That so? So how exactly did you wind up in the water?" Al asked, pulling up a chair. "Horse throw you?"

"Not exactly," I replied. "I fell off a cliff."

"Really? How'd you happen to manage that little feat?" he asked, leaning back.

"It's a long story," I replied.

"Well, seein' as how we're going to be here a

while, how about I put on a pot o' coffee and you can tell me all about it?"

"Coffee sounds great," I nodded.

"Wait till you taste it first. I ain't the best cook around," he chuckled.

"I've drunk from a buffalo wallow before. I'm sure it'll be fine."

"Why don't you start with what brought you to these parts," he suggested.

"What makes you think I ain't from around here, Al?" I asked.

"Well, for one thing, when you work in the theater long enough, you learn to pick up on accents, word use, and such," he explained. "Colorado, right?"

"Close enough," I replied.

"So why don't you start there."

The pot boiled as I recounted my story, while at the same time trying to remember everything I had overheard back on the trail.

"Al, did you ever notice how the worst experiences in life always seem to start off great, like everything was right with the world?" I asked.

"Seems like it often enough," Al replied in agreement.

"Well, that's how it all started. It was a beautiful day, especially for a sixteen-year-old boy and his cousin, riding the range with his pa. What I'm referring to happened a short while after Ma had passed some years back. For the longest period,

Pa just had no energy. It was as if all his spirit had left with her, and for months thereafter he did the chores around our ranch like he was one of the walking dead, or something. Never so much as a smile or a how-do-you-do to anyone. It almost broke my heart."

I couldn't help notice that Al developed a distant look. His eyes clouded up for a moment and he merely nodded at me. He understood all right.

"Then one day this letter came. It seems an old friend of Pa's, up in Wyoming, had recently come into some cash but, as he put it, was sorely horse poor. Needed about fifteen head of good stock and wouldn't trust nobody but my pa. He was willing to pay a fair price, but only if we could deliver the horses. It meant leaving the ranch for a spell, but that wasn't much of a problem since my sister Judith had recently married her old beau. Her new husband, Andy, had already started working on our ranch. They could tend to things well enough while we were gone, but my uncle Jake was out of town and Pa would need more help, if he was to herd those horses all the way up to Wyoming.

" 'Will, come over here. Son, how'd you like to ride with me a spell?' he asked me.

" 'Sure would, Pa,' I answered. I was eager enough. 'Where we headin'?'

" 'Oh, I figured you and I might just trot on up

to Wyoming with a few head,' he said, smiling at me. It was the first time I'd seen him grin in months.

" 'Wyoming!' I yelled. 'Oh boy.'

" 'I reckon we'll need to take your cousin Jimmy along, too. Jake asked me to keep an eye on him and he'd get pretty bored around here, hanging around with them newlyweds,' he said.

" 'Think it'll be all right with Uncle Jake?' I asked him.

" 'Thirteen is old enough to ride along with us, I guess. Besides, it'll be easier to keep an eye on him out on the trail. Better than having him stir up mischief around here.'

"I laughed out loud at that. 'He can be a handful I reckon, huh, Pa?' I said.

" 'No more than you at times I expect,' he replied teasing me.

"Once my pa got his mind set on doing something, he didn't stop moving. Not for a minute. There wasn't a whole lot of hurry up and wait in his nature. Two days later, he hand-picked the horses that he was willing to sell, packed the supplies we would need for the trip, and had already sent a telegraph to his friend in Wyoming, notifying him that we were on our way.

"We left on a Monday. I remember 'cause Pa refused to go along with Judy and her husband to church the day before. 'Too busy for the niceties,' was how he'd phrased it, but I expect it still had more to do with losing Ma.

"That morning we were saddled up early. Andy had promised he'd watch over the place and take care of everything. 'Not to worry, Mister Grayson, it'll be here when you return,' he said, then asked . . . 'By the way, when do you reckon that'll be?'

" 'The way I got it figured, it ought to take about three weeks to ride up there, trailing the herd, and about two weeks coming back,' he told Andy. 'And even if there are any problems, it shouldn't be no more than two months, at the most.' Pa looked over at Sis, and then back to Andy, saying . . . 'Now that you're married, I expect you ought to start calling me Pa, too, instead of Mister Grayson. Don't you think so, Judy?'

"She smiled back and nodded. Andy actually blushed. 'Thanks Pa,' he said, looking a little shy.

"Pa walked his horse over to Judy and smiled at her. Sis raised up on tiptoe to give him a kiss. Pa lifted her right up and gave her a big hug and kissed her back. 'I love you, honey,' he told her. Then, turning to my cousin, he added . . . 'At this time of year the weather should be on our side, Jimmy. Not too hot and not too cold.'

" 'Just like Goldilocks said,' Jimmy joked. 'Just right.' I just shook my head at him.

" 'Let's hope it stays that way,' he said. 'Guess you two better get 'em moving,' he said to both of us.

"My cousin and I grinned back, and then the three of us started off at a brisk walk.

" 'No sense running them all the way,' Pa warned us. 'We want them to arrive well muscled. Nobody pays for skin and bones. Right, boys?'

" 'Right!' my cousin and I shouted in unison.

"Judy and Andy waved us off, and, as we rode up the hill at the end of our property, Pa paused to take one last look and to wave, before cantering off.

"Over the next few days, we fell into a routine of sorts. Pa rode up ahead, guiding the herd, while Jimmy and I rode drag. We usually got up around five o'clock in the morning and, after a cup of coffee and some biscuits, were back in the saddle driving the herd toward Wyoming. It was hard riding, what with constantly cutting in and out, back and forth, trying to keep the horses bunched up and moving in a straight path. It was hard work, but Jimmy and I had never been happier. It was a great adventure, being out on the trail with Pa. He was constantly teaching, pointing out things like cloud patterns that might mean rain, or explaining how a horse's gait and the way he threw his head or dropped a shoulder when walking might indicate that he was favoring a lame leg. Pa showed us different animal tracks and talked about how the spacing between them might indicate the speed the animal was traveling. He taught us different ways to mark a trail and how to select the best place for a campsite. What he showed us were things you only learn with years of experience out in the open.

"Jimmy and I were doing more riding than we ever had before and went to bed each night bone tired. In spite of the aches and pains, we were happier than two kids in a candy shop. The air was fresh, the horses frisky, and there were none of the dull chores that Ma and Sis always made us do around the house. We didn't have to haul out the trash, or muck out the barn, and, once we were out of sight of the ranch, Pa relaxed some. With no womenfolk around, Jimmy and I didn't have to worry about minding our Ps and Qs. Well, at least not some of them.

"We were gone about a week and a half when Pa started acting a mite strange. He was always the quiet type, but suddenly he was more so. Jimmy was constantly asking him questions about this thing or that, but Pa usually answered him as best he could. That particular day, we were riding three abreast when Jimmy asked him whether or not we might meet up with any Injuns. I noticed my pa had started looking around, as if searching for something, and had totally ignored Jimmy's question. Pa favored my cousin Jimmy, and it wasn't like him to just ignore him. I was a mite worried that he had begun to dwell on Ma again, so I asked him if anything was wrong.

" 'Huh? Wrong? No, son, it's fine. I was just checking on something,' he told me. 'No need for you boys to worry.'

" 'What was it you were looking for, Uncle?' Jimmy asked.

"Pa looked around and sat up in his saddle while looking behind us.

" 'Looking for?' he said. He seemed absent-minded.

" 'Right, Pa,' I said. 'You mentioned you were checking for something.'

"Pa relaxed some and smiled back at me. 'Oh, nothing in particular. It just pays to stay on your toes out here. Never know when you might run into a grizzly or cougar or something that might carry off your cousin Jimmy here,' he joked.

" 'Very funny,' Jimmy said.

" 'No need to fret much on that, Pa,' I told him. 'He's too small and bony for them. They probably won't go for him. Not enough meat on his bones.'

" 'Hey!' Jimmy yelled, reaching across the saddle while taking a friendly swipe at me. 'I got enough to take you on.'

"Jimmy didn't notice anything wrong, but I saw it in Pa's eyes. Pa may have sounded like he was in better sprits, but his eyes kept darting around, and from that moment on he started riding in gradually larger circles around the herd, backtracking and such.

"Later that night Pa was pouring himself a cup of coffee when Jimmy, who was walking up behind him, carrying a saddle, tripped and fell. Pa dropped his cup, drew his pistol, and spun, moving faster than anyone I'd ever seen before. Jimmy was so surprised, he turned bleach white and just lay there, staring back. Pa uncocked his pistol and reholstered it. He then walked over to my cousin and helped him up.

" 'Sorry about that, boy, but you startled me.'

" 'I'll say he did,' I said. 'Told you he was clumsy,' I added, trying to lighten the mood. I knew, however, that there was something real bad bothering my pa. Over the next two days he kept up with the same behavior, restless and nervous-like. He took to separating from the herd for longer periods, and began riding circles around us as if he were looking for something. Trouble is, I just didn't know what it was that was bothering him, or how to help. Every time I asked him what the problem was, he merely said I was just imagining things, or claimed that he was looking for the next watering hole or something. Pa never lied to me before, but I had a nasty feeling in the pit of my stomach that he was now. Either that or he wasn't telling me the whole truth.

"One morning while we were preparing to break camp, Pa called us both over.

" 'Boys, I got something to tell ya. We aren't going to leave here just yet. I'm gonna ride ahead for a while and scout around. I want you boys to stay here.'

" 'Can I go with you, Uncle?' Jimmy asked. 'Willy can stay here and watch the herd. They seem pretty calm with all this grass around.'

"Pa looked distracted and just nodded. 'Yes, it is a good spot, but I want you to stay here with your cousin just the same. You boys, listen to me. I won't be gone more than three or four hours, but should something keep me a little longer than that, you just stay put.'

"The way Pa was explaining things somehow made me feel a little afraid.

" 'What sort of things might keep you, Pa?' I asked.

"He looked down at me and ran his hand through my hair. 'Oh, it's nothing to worry on, Will. I'm just being cautious, that's all. You never can be too careful out on the trail. Remember that. But if something was to delay me, say more than a whole day, and I'm not saying it will, I've drawn you this map for you to follow. It's pretty much a straight three-day drive from here on in.'

" 'Pa . . . ?'

" 'Don't fret on it, Will,' he interrupted me. 'I can take care of myself, can't I?'

" 'Sure, Pa,' I told him. 'If you can't there ain't nobody who can.'

" 'So we just sit here till you get back?' Jimmy asked.

" 'Don't expect you to just sit here,' Pa replied. 'You might spend some time curry-combing your mounts and checking their shoes. Always some work to do, too. Oh, and it wouldn't hurt, since you got some time, to saddle soap the leathers,' he added.

" 'Aw, Pa, can't we just keep going like we been doing?' I asked. 'I don't get it.'

" 'No!' he answered abruptly. 'You two do like I say now, hear?'

" 'Yes, sir,' we both promised him, and boy were we surprised at his intensity.

" 'And remember, anything longer than a day and you start the herd north like I told you.'

" 'And you'll catch up with us later, right, Pa?'

" 'Right, son,' he nodded. Suddenly he came over and gave me a big hug. 'You take care of Jimmy. I love you, boy.' It was comforting, but a rarity for him to show me so much emotion.

" 'I can take care of myself!' Jimmy argued angrily.

"Pa laughed and gave him a big hug as well. 'I'm betting you can, Jimmy.'

"He mounted up, and, as he turned to ride out, he gave one look back. 'Oh, one last thing, boys. Last night I cleaned and oiled your rifles. Will, you might remember to check that revolver of yours. Just don't shoot out the bore today.'

" 'Why not, Pa?' I asked, as our daily shooting lessons had been one of the highlights of our trip.

" 'No need to make too much noise,' he explained.

" 'Why not?' I asked, puzzled.

" 'Let's just say I don't want the horses to spook while I'm away.'

" 'All right, Pa, I won't.' I was even more puzzled now, since we had been shooting around these horses almost daily since they were foals.

" 'Anyone comes by when I'm away,' he paused, thinking a moment, 'you pull that pistol early and keep it at the ready. Don't let no one all the way into the camp. Hear me?'

" 'Got it, Pa,' I answered. Jimmy nodded as well.

" 'Take care, boys, and I'll see you soon.' He spurred his horse and took off at a lope."

I paused in the story while Al filled my cup with coffee.

CHAPTER TEN

I shifted my weight around before continuing with my story.

"We were camped in a small valley, lush with grass, and the herd was well settled. The last thing I remember was watching Pa ride over the crest of the hill. He paused to look back one last time, and as I waved to him he turned and disappeared from sight.

" 'Well, Jimmy,' I said, turning to my cousin, 'looks like it's just us trail hands now.'

" 'Reckon we should start on those chores your pa suggested?' he asked me.

"I thought about it a second, then told him . . . 'It'd give us something to do. Besides, you want to explain to him why we didn't get 'em done when he returns?'

"Jimmy let out a gasp and chuckled. 'Sure don't. Not me.'

" 'Not me, either,' I told him shaking my head. 'So let's get her done.'

"The rest of the morning passed fairly quickly, but around lunchtime I began to get a little antsy. Pa had said that he'd be gone a couple of hours, but that was around six in the morning. It was now well into the afternoon and there was still no sign of him. After lunch Jimmy must have noticed how nervous I was 'cause he offered to help clean up for me.

" 'You ain't had much to eat Will,' he commented.

" 'I'm worried about Pa,' I confessed to him.

" 'Oh, he's all right. Never met a man more capable,' he assured me, then added . . . 'Except my own pa, that is.'

"By four in the afternoon, I was more than just worried. I was downright afraid. Not for me, mind you, but for what might have happened to Pa. It wasn't like him to just ride off, and not at all like him to be late for something.

" 'You reckon we should get the herd moving in the morning, Will?' my cousin asked. 'That's what your pa said to do.'

"I'd given things a lot of thought since lunch. 'No, Jimmy, I reckon not,' I told him. 'The grazing's fine here and they'll stay put in this valley. You'll be fine.'

" 'What do you mean?' he asked.

" 'I mean I know my pa, and something's wrong. No way he'd be this late if he wasn't having some problem. I've got to go look for him.'

"He insisted he wanted to come, too.

" 'No you're not!' I told him.

" 'He's my uncle too you know,' he said. 'Just give me a reason why I can't go, and it better not be my age.'

" 'Look,' I told him, 'for one thing, we got a lot tied up in these horses and can't afford to lose them. You need to keep an eye on them. For another thing, I might miss him coming back. With you here to explain things, he won't worry as much when he returns.'

" 'I don't like it, Willy,' he said.

"I pushed my hat up on my forehead and looked back at him. I told him I didn't like it, either, but I had no choice. My pa should have been back by now, and I was worried.

"But Jimmy reminded me that Pa had told us to stay where we were, and then, if he didn't return, to take the horses north.

"I looked out at the horizon for any signs of a rider. There wasn't a sign of life.

" 'I know what he said and that's just what we'll do,' I told Jimmy. 'The only thing is that we are going to wait here a little longer, before we finally move out.'

" 'You mean *I'm* gonna wait here.'

"I nodded back at him and told him I was just going to look around, that I had to find out what happened. 'I'll be back in a day or so. Meanwhile, you just stay put. If I don't come back, either, then you leave the horses here and hightail it to that ranch we were headed to and tell them what happened. The herd should stay put here in the valley.'

"Jimmy started to protest, but I cut him short.

'I mean it, Jimmy. Stay put!' He looked up at me helplessly. I didn't want to hurt his feelings by mentioning his age, but he was only thirteen and small to boot. 'If anything bad happened to Pa that I can't handle, then there won't be anything you could do to help, either. Best thing you can do is go for more adults.'

" 'But what about you? What can you do?' he asked.

"I scratched my head. 'Guess that depends on what I find, don't it?'

"I saddled my palomino and rode out in the same direction as Pa had. After cresting the hill, I pulled my rifle from the scabbard and carried it. I didn't want Jimmy to see me pull it. It wouldn't help for him to be worrying any more than he already was. I knew my father and just couldn't imagine him falling off a horse or tangling with a bear. It had to be something far worse to stop Pa from keeping his word to return. I didn't know exactly what that was or how bad it could be, but I wasn't taking any chances. I knew it was going to be bad, whatever it was.

"I followed Pa's tracks like he taught me, and, after about two hours of riding, it started to get dark. I got off my horse and started leading him through a wooded area when I came across a mound of dirt that looked out of place. The leaves were bunched, but they weren't directly under a tree. The dirt was piled up, and yet there were no

118

signs of animals having scratched out a burrow or anything like that. I suddenly went all cold and got a painful tightening in my chest. Somehow or another I knew what I would find.

"After a quick look around to reassure myself that I was alone, I tied the horse to a nearby tree and walked slowly over to the mound. I dropped to one knee and reached down. I hesitated for a moment, afraid of what I would find, and then swept the leaves and dirt back to reveal a booted leg. I recognized the boot immediately. It belonged to Pa. I let out a cry and quickly cleaned the rest of the debris away. Pa had been killed and his body hastily covered up. I don't rightly know how long I stayed there, hugging him and crying, but eventually I let go and sat back.

"There was a bullet hole in his back. I looked around for signs, and noticed that Pa's holster was empty. I found the pistol under a nearby branch where it must have fallen or been thrown. It had been fired twice. I also noticed a trail of blood over some of the leaves leading to one of the tree trunks. From what I could make out, Pa had been jumped by three or four men but, in spite of that, had managed to get off a couple of shots. After killing my father, they must have dragged another wounded man up to the tree base in order to tend to him, and then later covered up the whole area.

"I reloaded Pa's pistol and stuck it in my belt

alongside mine. Pa wasn't carrying a shovel and I didn't have one, either, so I looked around for a heavy stick to dig a deeper hole. Afterwards I mounted my horse and rode him back and forth over the grave to wipe out any signs. I didn't want any wild animals digging it up later. That's when my sorrow turned to hatred.

"I followed the tracks of the killers for five hours, until I found their camp. I rode back a ways and tied up my horse so any sounds he might make wouldn't give me away. Then I started crawling until I was close enough to hear them talking.

"There were three men sitting around a semi-circle. I made very sure to stay low and out of sight in the bushes. Even though I was sure that the tracks had led me to these men, there was still some doubt in my mind. For one thing none of them seemed to be wounded. For another, they weren't acting particularly nervous. I decided to stay put and listen until dark so I could be sure of my prey. I remembered to keep my eyes off of the men. It was something my uncle had taught me from his days in the Army.

" 'Never stare at a man for too long, even if he can't see you,' he'd told me.

"When I asked him why, he had said . . . 'I believe it's because we all have a sort of sixth sense about such things. Don't truly know why it is, but, if you look square at a man you're

120

stalking for too long, he oftentimes gets jumpy and stares right back at you. Can sense you're there. Best to take quick peeks. Don't mean you can't use your other senses, though. Listening and such.'

"I did just that, lying still for a couple of hours or so until they finally lit a fire and started a pot of coffee brewing. That's when their conversation turned to the missing man.

" 'Too bad about Chris,' one of them remarked.

" 'His own damn fault,' another added. 'Shouldn't have moved in so quick, least ways not until he made sure the man was dead with a shot to the head. It was all the chance that guy needed to crank off a couple of rounds.'

" 'Never saw anyone draw, turn, and shoot so fast, and with two slugs in his back to boot,' the first one added.

" 'Think anyone will ever find him back there?' the third man asked, pointing with his coffee cup to a place near a large tree behind them.

" 'In this God-forsaken area? No way,' the first man said.

"Any doubts I might have had about these men were more than satisfied, not only by what I'd overheard, but also by my pa's Henry rifle that I saw lying on the ground next to the fire and by his horse, which I noticed tethered to a picket line with four others.

" 'So when do we go back for the herd?' one of

the men asked. Now that it was dark, I couldn't tell which one was talking.

" 'First thing in the morning,' another replied.

" 'What about the other hands?' the third asked.

"Someone laughed, then said . . . 'Hands? Kids, you mean. Ought to be easy.'

"I had seen and heard enough. I had planned to take my revenge, but it was now obvious I had to do so and end it that night, since by morning they'd be riding back to where Jimmy was camped. I crawled slowly backwards until I was sure they couldn't hear me. That's when I took a moment to plan my next move. I knew what I needed to do, but wasn't exactly sure of how best to go about it. After all, these three had killed my father and he was a better man than I was.

"I knew I couldn't just rush in shooting. I wanted to do it, but common sense told me that even with complete surprise I might not get all three, and the odds were against me coming out alive. I needed an edge and that's when I thought about my knife.

"I was big for my age, but lighting three men alone was not something I took lightly. There was never any doubt in my mind that I was going to kill them. I was too filled with hurt and anger to think of anything else. I wanted to level the odds some. I had always liked the dark. Most folks don't, and a lot are afraid of it, but not me. The more I thought about it, the more sense it made to use that to my advantage. I began smearing mud over my face and sticking leaves and branches to my clothes. When I was done you couldn't tell me from a bush. Only the thorn on this bush was a six-inch steel one.

"When I was sure I had camouflaged well enough, I started back toward their camp. I waited at the edge of the camp until they were all fast asleep, and then waited some more. I was cold right down to the soul, and patient as death itself.

"Once I thought the time was right, I started crawling toward the nearest man. I had listened to my uncle's war stories enough to know that when you crawl up on someone, you do it an inch at a time. Move and wait, move and wait. I already had my knife in hand so as not to make a noise by pulling it out at the last moment. Finally I was within inches of my prey and so began to draw back my arm to strike. That's when it hit me. Killing is one thing, but using a knife for it is so very cold, close and personal. I was only sixteen and had never killed before, other than hunting with a rifle. And even that was for food, not for trophy.

"When I looked down at that man's face I hesitated, and that was my mistake. Something must have startled him, maybe my breathing. I might have gasped, or maybe he just picked that moment to wake up. I don't know. All I know is he had great reflexes, and, as I started to strike, he rolled over and flung me off, yelling at the others to get the hell up. I rolled over, came up on one knee, and flipped the blade in my hand. I threw it with all my strength right at him. He sucked at least four inches of steel into his chest, screamed, and fell over dead. The other two had sprung up and started shooting. As luck would have it, they were firing in the wrong direction, The fires had died down and it was so dark they couldn't tell where I was. Kneeling down as I was and covered with mud and leaves, I looked like one of the bushes.

" 'What the hell's going on?' one of them yelled.

" 'You see anything?' the other asked.

" 'My God, he's dead,' one of them cried out.

" 'And so are you, you murdering son-of-a-bitch,' I yelled. By this time my Colt was in my hand and already cocked. I fired at the first target I found and rolled to my right. I came around and began unloading my pistol into both of them from a kneeling crouch. I fanned that six-shooter from right to left and back again until it was empty. I kept fanning it until the empty barrel revolved at least twice.

"I was shaking from both fear and anger. That, plus a whole lot of hatred to burn. Finally I just stopped and stood up. The three weren't moving, and I was fairly certain they weren't getting back up. I reloaded the Colt and retrieved the knife. I'd rather not talk about it, but let's just say that in my anger I made very sure all three were dead. Very dead.

"I wiped away some of the mud, and then picked up Pa's saddle with the Henry rifle and retrieved the horses. I took them all with me. The rustlers sure weren't going to need them any more. I thought about burying them for a moment, but decided it wasn't worth the effort. I opened Pa's saddlebag and removed a blank page from the ledger book he kept there. On it I wrote . . . Rustlers, Back shooters and Murderers. Just leave them be . . . And I left it near their bodies with a rock on top to keep it there.

"I rode back to where I had staked my palomino, and then headed back to find Jimmy's trail. After a day and a half of riding I found him and was never so glad to see anyone in my life. I'm sure after being left alone like that he felt the same. I told him what had happened without spelling out all the details, and then we rounded up the horses and headed north to finish the drive.

"Pa prided himself on being a good judge of character. His friend in Wyoming was no exception. Richard Barnes was his name, and he took us in and helped us restock for the trip back. There was never a second thought on his part about paying the price agreed upon, either. He didn't even hesitate and paid us in cash, right on the spot. That's when I knew I could trust him. We stayed only two days, and then started back. Mister Barnes offered to send another man along to accompany us, but I turned the offer down.

" 'We made it this far, I reckon we can get back all right,' I told him.

"He pushed his hat brim up and nodded. 'After what you done,' he said to me, 'I reckon you're man enough.' He put an arm on my shoulder. 'William, your pa was a good man,' he added. 'One of the best friends I ever had.'

"I thanked him for all he had done for us, including giving us supplies for the trip back and he told me it was the least he could do. Then he told us to take care and, if we were ever in these parts again to look him up.

" 'It's a promise,' I told him, and then Jimmy and I rode out. I wasn't looking forward to telling my sister what had happened, but it had to be done.

"By the time we arrived back home, Sis and her husband Andy were settled into their own routine and the place looked fine. When my uncle got back, we discussed going back for Pa's body and returning him home. Uncle Jake thought about it a while and disagreed. 'Knowing your pa, he's fine just where he is. Hell, only reason he ever gave up the trail was for your ma, and she's gone. No reason to disturb him. He's restin' peacefully now that his family is safe. Best leave it be.'

"I'd made my mind up soon after that to leave home for good. There were too many old memories at the ranch and not enough new ones to suit me, if you know what I mean." Al Kleiner sipped his coffee and just nodded back at me as if he was mulling things over.

"When I told Judith and Andy of my plans, they objected. They insisted the place was rightfully half mine.

"I just shook my head. 'I'm taking Pa's Henry rifle, his saddle, my stallion, some supplies, and an extra pack horse,' I told them. 'That's all I'll need. You keep the place with my best wishes.' I mounted up and took a last look around. Good place to raise a family, I noted, then turned and rode out.

"I spent the next couple of years trying not to gather moss, picking up work wherever I could find it. I drove cattle, rode shotgun for a while, and even dealt faro for a summer. Finally I worked my way up to Bannock, where the gold mines were, and tried my luck at digging for a living. But as luck would have it, whenever there is money available, a reason pops up to spend it. My sister needed cash to pay off the mortgage on the bank, so I rode into Blue Lake Ridge to send it to her and that's when I got waylaid.

"I don't know if they were trying to rob me or had something more sinister in mind right from the git go, but I found myself thrown sideways over a saddle and being taken out of town, to be put away for good. I figured the only way out was to fling myself over the cliff and into the water. It was a touch farther down than I expected, though. Next thing I know, I'm lying in your cot inside this cabin."

Al had listened quietly through the whole story, but he finally spoke up. "Something just don't make much sense," he said.

"What's that?" I asked.

"Well, for one thing, if they was just interested in robbing you, how come they didn't just leave you there in the alley once they rolled you?"

"I don't know . . . it doesn't make much sense," I agreed. "I had more money, but not on me, and they didn't know where I'd stashed it. Hell, I'm not even sure they knew how much I had."

"Maybe they were taking you out to rough you up. You know . . . to get you to tell them where the rest of the gold was."

I tried hard to remember the conversation I'd overheard on the trail that night.

I shook my head. "You know, Al, from what I recall, it seems to me they thought I was already dead. They sounded more interested in my horse than me."

"Maybe when they went to rob you, they hit you so hard they thought they'd killed you and were just making sure by hiding the body," Al suggested.

"Maybe. Things are still a little blurred, but it just don't make sense to me that way. They could just have easily left me in the alleyway. Besides, I seem to recall them saying something like they were going to kill me, if I wasn't already dead."

"Could they have been talking about killing you after finding out about the gold?"

"Could be, but for some reason I doubt it."

Al stretched and stood up. "Maybe you best let it rest for now. I'll fix us up some grub, and then you best take another nap and let your body heal. I'll work on this here puzzle, too. Between the two of us we might come up with something."

"Some food'd be great. I can't thank you enough."

Al laughed. "You ain't tasted my cooking yet."

CHAPTER ELEVEN

The next morning when I awoke, I found my new friend already up with a full pot of brew that, he truthfully admitted, ought to be ashamed to call itself coffee. He was sitting at the table, across the cabin, wrapping some strips of cloth around a long branch.

"What're you up to old-timer?" I asked, wiping the sleep from my eyes.

"Been thinking on things some. You know, Will, I consider myself a pretty good judge of character. Through the years, as an actor, I've come across a bunch of con artists, flim-flam men, and such. But I trust you. You don't strike me as the sort to ride the owl hoot trail."

"Don't be so sure. I might be capable of more than I told you," I answered truthfully.

Al laughed and slapped his knee. "Don't get your feathers in a flap. I ain't saying you ain't tough as rawhide. Shoot, surviving that fall told me that." I smiled to myself as he continued. "It's just that I meant that I believe your story. Hell, you got to be the poorest excuse for a ruffian I ever did see. You could never fool me into believing you ain't right."

"Why not?" I asked, somewhat angered. It

sounded to me like he was describing a goody two-shoes.

"How many bad men you know who would ride hundreds of miles out of their way to send money back to a brother-in-law?" he stated, and laughed.

He had a point. "Fine. So me and George Washington don't tell no lies," I answered angrily. After all, I hadn't had my coffee yet.

"Hell, Washington was a President," he said, shaking his head, "so even he told a few whoppers. He just knew how to get away with it, is all. And I can teach you that, too, sure enough."

"You gonna teach me some of that actin' stuff?" I asked.

"Sure, I will. Might be fun. Haven't had much company for quite a long while now." His gaze drifted, and it seemed to me he was remembering something unpleasant.

"So what's up with the stick?" I asked, pointing to the branch he was working on.

"Well, the way I figure it, we got to gather more information on what's what. You can't go into town . . . not with that bum leg of yours . . . so I'll have to. Meanwhile, I found this forked stick to make a crutch out of. Been wrapping some rags around the top so you can rest your arm on it without rubbing yourself raw. You can get around with this till I get back."

I was truly touched. Not many would go to so

much trouble for a total stranger. "I don't know what to say, Al. I sure owe you one."

"We'll see about that later. For now, try to remember anything else you might have forgotten. Meanwhile, I'll head into town and mosey around. We can start our acting lessons when I get back."

Al left for town the next morning. My ankle was still swollen and my shoulder was tied up in a sling, so I was glad to have that makeshift crutch to get around on. Rather than remain cooped up, I went out to explore the surroundings. The previous night Al mentioned that he had wandered onto the place about two years earlier. Since he had found it completely deserted, he moved in and just made himself at home.

After a quick look around, I decided the cabin might originally have been a line shack. Perhaps someone had thought in terms of eventually starting a relay station, or it might have been the beginnings of a homestead that, for some reason, the owner had later abandoned. At any rate, I couldn't find much left on the property of any interest other than the basics.

There was a pole barn of sorts, which in reality was nothing more than a big lean-to. It was constructed of a couple of old logs that were nailed together, at a forty-five degree angle, to a back wall made of planks. At the far end, between the logs, was a feed trough, and the floor was covered in dirt and straw. There was room for three horses to be tied, standing up, but, as far I could tell, Al only had the one sway-back old Grulla, which he had ridden to town, and a small-size burro that he had left behind. Before leaving, he introduced me to Crackers, his Colorado Mockingbird, noting that she had a tendency to bite and kick if she got her dander up. "She goes crackers on me from time to time, so it seemed like a good name," he'd joked. I patted the burro on the rump and, using an old wooden pitchfork, shoveled some hay into her stall. She gave me a suspicious look for a moment, and then lowered her head and began eating.

Around back I also found a long irrigation trench that led to a well of sorts on the far side of the cabin, and a large work box with an assortment of rusted tools. Later, I would clean and sharpen them, but for now there was something else that attracted my attention. I noticed several of the trees out back with large patches of moss growing on them, and there were several varieties of herbs growing around that I could use.

Back home my ma was the local healer, and she took to teaching my sister Judith at an early age all about herbal cures, potions, and such. I was too busy chasing squirrels or hunting deer to pay too much attention to most of their goings on, but

Judy always managed to corral me into letting her practice on me. I guess some of it must have rubbed off, because the sight of that moss reminded me of a poultice Ma and Sis used to fix for Pa from time to time when he had an ache or pain.

After collecting what I needed, I heated up some water, mixed the herbs in with some mud from behind the cabin, packed the mash around my sore ankle, and covered it with the moss. I then wrapped some strips of cloth around the moss and tied it all down. I put some on my shoulder too. It all itched like the devil for a day or two, but the swelling went down almost immediately, and the pain was much less than it had been. With the help of the crutch, I was able to get around pretty well and began the work I'd promised myself to do in order to repay Al for his trust in me.

From the amount of dust and debris in the cabin, I could tell Al wasn't much for doing chores, so over the next few days, once I was feeling up to it, I hammered, filed, drilled, swept, and dusted till the place looked clean enough for the Queen of Sheba. I repaired loose hinges and fixed some broken panels in the cabin. It was one way to repay a favor, but mostly it was a way to pass the time. Whenever I wasn't working, my mind got to thinking on that beating I had gotten in the alley and the men who were all set to kill me. All that thinking, without being able to do anything about it, was giving my stomach the colic. The work took my mind off of things and helped me forget my aches and pains, not to mention my anger.

On the afternoon of the sixth day since Al had left for town, I was mucking out the lean-to when I heard a twig snap. I shifted my weight off my bad leg and slowly removed the holster thong off my pistol hammer. The instant I heard another noise I spun and drew, right into the nose of Al's Grulla. I stared at him in shock. Replacing the Colt, I just shook my head in amazement.

"You nearly scared the daylights out of me, Al," I said.

"Didn't do my heart any good, either, son. That was a mighty fast draw, though. Your ribs must be a lot better. Not using the sling any more, either, I see."

I rolled my left shoulder around. "Much better, thanks. That swayback sure walks soft, don't she?"

"Not much to look at, but she treads lightly. Used to belong to a fur trapper who spent a lot of time in Injun territory. Couldn't afford a lot of noise, iffen you get my drift."

I nodded. "I can see where she might come in handy."

Al dismounted, pulled the saddle and bridle,

and, pointing the horse to the trough, gave her a whack on the rump. He tossed his saddlebags over his shoulder, looked around the place, and whistled. "You been a busy little beaver haven't you, lad?"

"A way to pass the time, that's all," I replied.

"Well, thanks all the same," he answered, shaking my hand.

"Find out anything interesting, Al?" I asked.

"Sure did," he replied. "I also brought some more coffee with me from town. Let's go in and have some and I'll tell you all about it."

"Great, but, if you don't mind, since I went to the trouble of cleaning the pot, why don't you let me fix the coffee this time?"

"Sounds good to me," he said, and laughed. "Let's go."

Once he had settled in and found his pipe, Al began to recount his trip to town. "Well, now, where to begin?" he said, clearing his throat.

"Why not at the beginning, Al?" I joked. "That's usually a good place to start."

Al raised his eyebrows. "You sound like a theater critic," he said, laughing.

"Sorry," I replied, sipping my coffee.

"As I was saying . . . before I was so rudely interrupted," he continued, "I found out quite a bit. See, I figure there's always two places in any town where folks are likely to have a loose tongue."

136

"The saloon," I offered.

"Right," he said, "and the other is the local shebang."

I was forced to chuckle at Al's reference to the general store.

"What's so funny?" he asked.

"That's what my uncle Jake always called our local emporium, back home. Said it came from the Gaelic word Sheehan, meaning to speak easy."

"Don't rightly know about that," Al replied, shrugging, "but there's a mercantile in town and folks seem to speak pretty freely while in there." He tapped his pipe absent-mindedly on his boot and, taking a pouch from his pocket, began to refill it with tobacco.

"So what'd they have to say?" I asked, almost as much out of desperation to get his story going as out of curiosity.

Al finished lighting his pipe. "Well, for one thing the bank's been robbed," he said, taking a deep puff. "Whole town's riled up about it."

I looked up in surprise. "Really? When was that?"

"About the same time you got dumped in the pond. It happened over the week-end of the town's holiday celebration. The manager found all the money gone when the bank reopened on Tuesday."

"They got any idea who done it?" I asked.

"Sure do," he answered, taking another pull on his pipe and reaching for his coffee cup.

"Well . . . who was it?" It seemed to me that Al liked to drag things out for effect, but I found it nerve-racking.

"You did," he answered.

"*What?* Me? How could I?" I asked.

Al smiled. "I didn't say you could, just that the folks in town think you did."

I was dumbfounded. "Why would they think that, Al? Why me?"

He blew a smoke ring and stared off as if pondering his reply. "Well, apparently you got a reputation in town as a troublemaker. You know . . . the kind who's generally a lightning rod for violence, what with causing two fights and a shooting in just one day."

I just shrugged my shoulders, but admittedly I could see how a reputation like that might have started easily enough.

"Then there were the witnesses," he added.

"Witnesses?" I said, angry now. "How could there be any witnesses. Who were they and what did they have to say about me?" I was fuming.

"A couple of them was in the saloon when you had your little display of pistol craft. Some others were at the assay office or out in front, on the street, when you come a-tumbling out, fists a-flying."

"That it? That doesn't prove anything," I argued.

"No, but, as we say in the theater, it goes to character development," he replied.

"Anything else?"

"Well, there was that feller from the livery stable. Claims you barreled out of there late at night without paying your bill, and he said he noticed you had several extra saddle-bags thrown over the horse, both front and back. Said they looked mighty heavy in his opinion."

"That so, huh? You don't believe him do you, Al?" I asked, feeling a little worried.

"Well, I reckon you could have gotten thrown from your horse trying to escape from town, and then fallen over the cliff," he said, pausing to tamp down the tobacco in his pipe. "But, no, son, I don't think you did it. You just don't seem the type. That, plus there's some things that just don't add up in my mind."

"Thanks for that, Al," I said, relaxing some. "So what doesn't add up?"

He stared off into space again. "Well, for one thing, if you were going to rob a bank, it seems to me you'd lay low first and not draw all that attention to yourself beforehand like you done while in town."

"Anything else?"

He looked back at me and nodded. "If we go

on the assumption that you're innocent, then it stands to reason what you told me about meeting up with that Elliott woman is also true," he explained.

"It is. Count on it. So, is she all right? Anything happen to her after I got waylaid in that alleyway?"

"Seems to be just fine," Al replied, smiling. "Might pretty, too, I might add."

"She is that," I said, nodding in agreement.

"And the good news is, she hasn't left town," he added.

I looked up at him.

"Yep, she's still there. What's more, she's become real cozy-like with the town sheriff," he said.

"Then she should have told him what happened to me in the alley. Surely she'd know it couldn't have been me that robbed the bank."

"Doesn't seem like things worked out that way. The way I heard it, she claims you offered to accompany her toward the livery, and then took a short cut all by your lonesome down a side street."

"Right so far"—I nodded—"more or less."

"Then according to her story," Al continued, "you just disappeared. She said she waited for you in the street a good while, and then went down the alleyway, but there was no sign of you. So she just went on alone."

"They must have dragged me off by then," I offered. "But didn't the sheriff find that suspicious?"

Al agreed with me, but not exactly like I meant. "He did find it suspicious. In fact, the sheriff was the one who made sure that the posse went out especially lookin' for you," he explained. "See, he believes you disappeared to go off and rob the bank."

"She didn't see or hear anything strange when I got smacked?" I asked.

Al shook his head. "Apparently not. Least ways not according to what folks are sayin'. A puzzlement, ain't it? You figure she's lying?"

I thought about it and shrugged. "Nah, I guess not. It doesn't figure. What would a widow lady get out of it?"

"Besides the money you mean?" he asked. "Some sort of a grudge?"

"She didn't even know me that well. Hell, she got off the stage that very same day. She wouldn't have anything against me personally, and I doubt she would have had enough time to plan a bank robbery in that short a period," I said, puzzling over the whole thing.

"Supposedly you had enough time to do the robbery and you were only there one day," he commented.

"Except I didn't do it," I pointed out.

"You reckon she could be in cahoots with

someone else?" Al asked. Thinking it over, he then scratched his head. "Naw, that doesn't figure, either. Iffen she was part of the robbery, why would she hang around town afterward? Two stages left since then. And one thing's for certain, it sure as hell doesn't make sense to be making time with the town sheriff if she was involved in the robbery. Much too risky. It'd be crazy."

"I agree, but why wasn't she worried about what happened to me?" I asked, becoming more puzzled than ever.

"Sort of seems like she was. After all, she waited a fair while for you to come back out of that alley for her, and then went in looking for you. For a lady alone at night that took some guts," he remarked.

"Guess so," I admitted.

"At any rate, once the sheriff explained his theory about the bank robbery, you probably leapt clear out of her mind. Why should she be concerned with a bank robber, who has no future, when there's an eligible lawman around?"

I had to admit he had a point.

"Hell, he probably made you look like the kind of low-life who would abandon a lady, alone at night, without giving it a second thought," he added.

I remembered how quickly Sheriff Kent had cut in on me, once he got a good look at her. I wouldn't put it past him to paint as bad a picture of his competition as possible. "Anything else? Anything a little more positive?" I asked hopefully.

Al shook his head. "Couldn't find out much more about her. All the folks in town are talking about is how much she and the sheriff been going together, all hot and heavy, since she hit town. Some don't think it real proper for a widow lady to get back in action so soon. Personally I don't see how it matters much. Maybe she's just set her sights on a new husband. You know, maybe she's the kind that doesn't want to be alone. There are women like that, you know."

"I suppose. Someone that good-looking ain't gonna be alone long, that's for sure," I remarked. Then, suddenly recalling something else: "Hey, wait. How about those three cowboys I had the run-in with in the bar. Maybe they had something to do with it?"

"Apparently not," Al said, shaking his head. "After they dried out and the doc finished patching them up, they left town lickety-split. Sheriff made sure of that."

"When was that?" I asked, trying my best to solve this puzzle.

"It was later that same day . . . before the bank was robbed."

"They could have doubled back," I suggested.

"Nope. Word is they went back to their outfit. After the robbery, the posse caught up with their herd and they was vouched for by the trail boss. Sheriff Kent checked it out. Even had his men search the chuck wagon. Way it appears, you were the only suspicious one anybody claims to have seen that night. Whoever pulled this job made a clean getaway. And apparently you're supposed to be a red herring. It's just too bad for you the folks in town don't know that."

"It's gonna be too bad for that gang, whoever they are," I answered angrily. "Herring's supposed to wind up dead, cooked, and served on a plate red or otherwise. Instead, this fish is going back a shark. Trust me, when I find out who framed me, I'm gonna eat 'em alive."

"If you find them," Al reminded me.

I considered his remark. "How much do you know about this town's lawman?" I asked.

"Not much," he answered. "Folks seem to like him well enough. Hasn't been sheriff very long . . . only a couple of months. The previous sheriff was found dead, inside the cattle pen just outside of town. Supposedly he was investigating a theft. Everyone figures he must have fallen, and then gotten kicked or stomped to death. Kent came along a little after that and applied for the job. Took to the town right off and visa versa. Why do you ask?" Al said as he poured himself another cup of coffee.

"I want to know if he's the sort someone can reason with? Even though we got off on the wrong foot, maybe you could set things up so we could meet somewhere and parlay. If I can get him alone and explain things, I might make him believe me . . . maybe he'll give me half a chance. Think he'd be of help?"

Al shook his head. "Iffen he sees you first, then he'll be the last thing you'll ever see."

"How's that?"

"I forgot to mention one little thing," he added, noticing the fire going out in his pipe bowl.

"What?" I asked.

"The bank has a Wanted Dead or Alive poster out on you. The town lost a lot of money, including the sheriff. He said if he sees you, he's going to shoot first and ask questions later. The folks in town is all riled up. Seems like anyone asking questions or offering any other theory about the robbery is put down right quick like. The sheriff and the folks on that posse done made up their mind and the whole town has too."

"That's what you call one little thing?" I replied, feeling irked.

Al didn't answer. He merely shrugged, struck a lucifer, relit his tobacco, and went back to puffing on his pipe. I took another swig of coffee, but this time it was a little harder going down.

CHAPTER TWELVE

I spent the rest of the morning mulling over everything the old-timer had told me. After a while, I came to the conclusion that I would have to go to town and see for myself how things really stacked up.

"I don't see any way around it, Al. I've got to get into Blue Lake Ridge," I said.

"I'm a-tellin' you, son, they'd sooner shoot you as hang you, iffen they were to get half a chance," he said. "So why don't you just hightail it for the far and yonder and not look back?"

"Wish I could, Al, but there's a couple of reasons I've got to do this," I replied.

"Are these reasons important enough to get yourself killed over?" he asked.

"For one thing, my sister's still in trouble and needs the money I hid back in town."

After considering what I'd said, he nodded. "All right, I'll give you that. What's the other?"

"Well"—I considered my reply carefully—"I won't run like a scared dog. I just won't do it. Especially when I'm not to blame for something. Besides, I don't want to spend the rest of my life, looking over my shoulder, worried that some bounty hunter's after me. I figure I've got to clear my name or die trying. So I need to get real clever, but quick. I have to think up some way to safely get into town, and then go after those low-life dry gulching s.o.b.'s."

"But you don't even know who they are, where they are, or what they look like," Al pointed out. "They probably aren't even in the territory. Most likely they're long gone by now."

"I think I have enough to go on. Or at very least there's a direction for me to get started looking in," I said. "I just need to figure out how to keep from getting shot as soon as I hit town."

"Well, maybe iffen we put our heads together we can come up with something," Al suggested.

"Nothing seems to come to mind, right now," I answered, shaking my head. It was then that I noticed what looked like part of a book sticking out from one of his trunks. I always was one for reading anything I came upon. Ma put that notion into me when I was knee-high. I was getting myself all worked up, and being cooped up so long in Al's cabin had already made me edgy. I thought maybe reading something would take my mind off my troubles, sort of help clear out the cobwebs. "That a reading book over there?" I asked, pointing to the trunk.

"Sort off. Actually, it's one of those new Beadle dime magazines from back east. Picked it up a while back. Read it cover to cover several times. You're welcome to it. This one's supposed to be full of true adventure stories. One in there I

147

especially liked was all about a fellow called the Masked Avenger."

I shook my head. "Never heard of him."

"He was supposed to have lived a long time ago. Used to get dressed up in this mask and have sword fights with evil aristocrats. Sort of a Robin Hood with a German accent."

"Aristo-whats?" I asked, confused.

"You know, them rich folks what run Europe," he explained. "Think they're born better than everyone else. This Avenger fellow went around fighting them in order to help the common folk."

"Why the mask?" I asked.

"To disguise himself, of course." Al seemed to pause a moment in thought. "Say, now, there's an idea. Why don't you use a disguise? Might just get you safely back into town."

"Oh, sure, I can see it now," I said. "I go riding into a town that's just had its bank robbed, wearing a mask. Seriously, Al, how far do you suppose I'll get before half the town blows me out of my kack? A masked rider?" I laughed and shook my head at such a fool notion.

"Oh, the arrogance of youth," Al replied angrily. "Always thinking that just because someone's older, they must be addled or off their rocker. Look, young man, my get up and go may have got up and went, but I still have my mind left. I wasn't referring to you wearing a mask, you young whippersnapper."

"Whoa there, ol' hoss. Look, I'm sorry," I said. "I just can't follow your track."

"Well, then, pipe down and listen. Remember when I said I was an actor," he asked.

"*Lion of the West.* Right. Got it. So?"

"Think about it. What is it actors are good at?" he asked.

"Talking all the time and trying to tell other folks how to vote?" I answered, laughing.

Al threw an old boot at me and I was forced to duck. "No, you idiot," he chastised. "I mean disguises and costumes and such! An actor's got to learn how to change his appearance so that people believe he is someone else. See what I'm a-getting at?"

I thought about it a moment and nodded. He did have a point, and it triggered a long-forgotten memory from my childhood.

"Now that you mention it, Al, I do remember my pa telling me a story about my great grandfather. He used to ride with Francis Marion," I began.

"The Swamp Fox of the Revolution?" Al asked.

"The very same. Anyway, seems as how Colonel Marion and my great grandpappy once stole some uniforms from a British supply house. Then one night they simply walked right into a British dinner party, proud as peacocks, and proceeded to share food and drink with them redcoats. Heard all about their plans for the next battle and everything."

"Sounds good," Al said. "So how can we use that?"

I started to think on it, but, try as I might, I couldn't seem to make things work. "Now that I hear it out loud, I guess it won't work," I said, shaking my head.

"Why not?"

"Well, for one thing I can't just change into a new coat and walk into town. Like you said, I don't know who the gang members are or what they look like. Hell, I don't even know if there are any left in town. But rest assured, Al, if there are, they'd recognize me at first sight. Probably plug me before I got ten paces. And besides the gang members, there are a few other folks in town who'll remember me. I'll bet they all had money in that bank, too."

"Even so, it might still work," Al said after some thought.

"How so?" I asked hopefully.

"You aren't listening to me too good, son," Al replied.

"What do you mean?"

"Remember me telling you about how an actor has to sort of become a whole other person? Well, he doesn't do it just by changing a coat. You've got to change the way you look, the way you walk, and even the way you talk. Here, I'll show you."

Al opened the trunk in the corner, turned his

back on me, and started to pull things out from the box. "Don't look at me for a moment," he warned. "Just close your eyes and don't open them till I say so."

I went along with him and shut my eyes.

"All right, you can open them now," he said.

I looked up. It was truly amazing. In the corner, instead of old Al, grizzled and rickety, there stood a full-fledged mountain man, complete with buckskins, powder horn, and 'coon-skin cap. But more than that, Al's whole face was different, younger somehow. His hair was a different color, his nose had changed, and, when he walked around the room, he was more erect and had a sort of swagger. It was truly like being in the cabin with a total stranger.

"That you, Al?" I asked, surprised.

He laughed. "The name's Crockett, but you can call me Davy. I done kilt me more b'ars than the sky's got stars and some say there ain't enough moonshine in ol' Kentuck' to even begin to wet my whistle. I'm half man, half mountain lion, and all American." This was stated as he walked back and forth along the wall in front of me.

"I am truly astonished!" I cried. "Think you could teach me some of that actin' stuff?"

"Sure I could. Why, acting ain't all that hard. It's sort of like play pretending but for real. The trick in your case is going to be to find a real good disguise." He looked me over for a moment with his hand stroking his chin.

"Opposites, that's the trick," he suddenly proclaimed.

"What's that you're saying?" I asked.

"See, iffen you want to fool folks, you got to undo what they see. If someone is old, they got to make the audience see young. Too much hair, make 'em see bald. You get it?" he said.

"Yeah, I see."

"Well, take you for example. You're tall, young, and got that big moustache."

All of a sudden I didn't like where this conversation was going. My hand made its way slowly up to my face. "So?" I asked.

"So, we make you look old and wrinkled and get rid of that fancy lip hair," he replied.

"Great," I moaned. "Then what?" I was almost afraid to ask.

"Well, now, let's see what we got." Al turned back to his trunk and began pulling out clothes and an assortment of hats. He reached in and removed a tri-point hat and eye patch. "Pirate? Nope, no good, not enough water," he mumbled. "Hunchback? Nah, I don't think so," he mumbled to himself more than to me.

An Injun feather bonnet was next and produced the same response. "Nope, don't want to start a war, just sneak you into town." A corset, wig, and ladies umbrella was produced next, but I had only to scowl and shake my head firmly for him to get the message.

"How about a rich, good looking gambler?" I suggested.

"Try to think inconspicuous, lad," he said, his head still focused on what was in the trunks.

"Incon-what?"

"Means we don't want to attract attention, lad. You need to blend in, not stand out." Al pulled out some tins and a clump of what looked like white hair and straightened up. Looking me over, he noticed the crutch and smiled. "That's it!" he exclaimed.

"What's it, Al?" I asked. "You mind letting me in on all this?"

"See, you're tall, straight, and strong. That's the first thing people notice."

I smiled. "Comes with living, right? Nothing wrong with that, is there?"

Al shook his head in disgust. "There is if you don't want to be noticed. You trying to win a beauty contest or get yourself lynched?" he asked, wagging a finger at me.

"I see your point," I answered.

"Now that crutch there might be just the thing we need. It'll double you over, make you lame and feeble and give you some age and surprise, you'll be . . ."

"Inconspicuous?" I finished for him.

"Right. Now you're getting the idea. Say,

didn't I hear you mention that you did a little prospecting?"

I nodded my head. "You could say that."

Al grinned and slapped his knee. "You know I think I got just the bit. Even got Crackers to go with it. Nobody's ever seen her."

Over the next few days, we practiced what Al called getting into character. I learned how to cackle like an old geezer, how to shuffle my feet when I walked, and how to bend over, bracing myself on the top of the crutch, which made me look older and weaker. The funny thing is, by this time my ankle was almost back to normal. I now had to use a crutch I really didn't need. At least for walking around that is.

Al began teaching me how to put on show make-up, using some sticky glue from his tins to add clumps of white hair to my eyebrows and sideburns. He had me put my own hair into a net of sorts from his show trunk and added on a white wig that was stringy and sparse on top. It made me look like I was bald. I also had to shave off my moustache, which I guess was the hardest part. Later, he used some rubbery substance to add wrinkles to my face. By the time he was finished, I looked old enough to be his father. Felt that way, too.

"Take a look, old-timer," he said, holding up a mirror.

The face that reflected back at me was a total stranger. The nose was more beak-like, and there were enough wrinkles to keep a maid ironing for a month.

"Wow! Is that what I'm going to look like when I'm your age, Al?"

He looked at me angrily, shook his head, and replied: "Naw, I prettied you up some. You'll likely be much uglier by then. Now walk around and get a feel for the part. Go get Crackers and act like you're heading into town after a long spell of digging for color in hot dirt."

"Got it," I said, hobbling out the cabin door. I unhitched Al's Colorado mockingbird, all the while trying very hard not to get bit in the process, and began leading Crackers around the cabin. I was cackling and talking to myself the whole time. It was kind of fun, this acting thing, and I was becoming real pleased with myself and how much I'd learned in such a short time when Al suddenly called me back.

"Hey, Grayson!" Al shouted. "Will Grayson!"

I turned around. "Yeah, Al, what is it?"

He looked both angry and frustrated. "No, you dog-goned bonehead!" he yelled. "How many times I got to tell you? Don't fall for that one. iffen anyone recognizes you, or uses your name, you ain't you. Remember? You're someone else. Supposed to be this old prospector feller. Understand?"

"Oh, yeah . . . you're right. Sorry," I replied sheepishly.

"Sorry don't cut it. This ain't opening night, son, this here's your life we're talking about. One stupid mistake like that, iffen they find you out, well, then, my new apprentice is a goner."

"Don't worry, Al, I'll get it right."

"You better. Here, let's go over that shuffle again and the voice change one more time."

CHAPTER THIRTEEN

That night, after dinner, Al and I sat outside the cabin enjoying the night air. It was so peaceful you'd never know there was a care in the world. Al was puffing away on his pipe and had a sorrowful look on his face.

"My ma used to say 'I'll give a penny for your thoughts,' " I commented.

Al looked over at me.

"Don't get me wrong, Al, I'm not usually one to butt into a man's private time, but you look like something's really bothering you."

"Nothing special, son," he replied. "It's just the memories that catch up with a feller from time to time."

Al was such a sociable sort, what with his acting and all that, I found it strange he'd ended up in a secluded place like this. I swept my hand in an arc around the cabin. "Not that I mind the quiet, Al, but you have to admit this place is a mite out of the way. Mind telling me how you ended up here?"

He looked at me without answering for a while. Then he looked down at his pipe and tapped the bowl on the edge of the chair. He pulled out a tobacco pouch from his shirt pocket and refilled the pipe. "No, I suppose not," he finally replied.

"Ain't talked much about it for a long, long time. See I wasn't always like this. A loner, I mean. When I was younger, I was a real fire-burner, eager to prove myself to the world. In a very short time, I went from a young upstart farm boy in Illinois to a real big shot on the stages back east."

"I remember you mentioning that," I said.

"Well, I had to keep proving myself. Had to have more and bigger audiences. Truth is, there ain't an actor alive who hasn't had ups and downs. I accepted that. It's part of the learning process.

"Over the years, I've waited tables, done some carpentry, and even drove a stage once."

"I did, too," I noted.

"Did it all and just tacked it up to experiences that would help me mature as an actor. I considered myself quite an artist. I took my craft real seriously. Too seriously some might say."

"How so?" I asked.

"Well," he said, relighting his pipe, "you know how it is, all work and no play. Never had time for a real social life. Turns out that's the most important experience of all. I was so busy playing roles about other people's lives, I never had time for one of my own. By the time I found that out, I was getting a mite long in the tooth."

"But not too long," I suggested.

He chuckled. "Right, not too long. Then one

day I took a job with a traveling show. Only reason I did it was to get to Denver where they had bigger shows."

I interrupted his story. "Mind if I guess? She was part of the traveling show. Whoever she was."

His eyes turned hard for an instant, then he relaxed. "Right. Her name was Marjory and she was the daughter of the show's owner. He played piano and she sang and danced. She was twenty-five and I was thirty-nine, and we fell hard for each other. I stayed on with the show for a year and forgot all about Denver. Eventually we were married and after a while she told me she was with child."

"Sounds fine so far. So what went wrong," I pursued.

"Well, that was the happiest time of my life, but then after a spell I got the same old conquer-the-world itch and I just had to scratch it. So, then we received two job offers. One was down South and another up North. The Southern job was an easier trip and the weather would likely have gone easier on us, especially with Majory being pregnant and all."

"But you chose to go North," I guessed.

He hung his head down and nodded. A tear began to form in his eye. "It was a bigger opportunity, professionally, for me. Not for my father-in-law or for the show, mind you, just for me. I rationalized it all by saying the money would be better and that it would help us out once the child was born. But the truth is, I was risking her for my own ego. Seeking fame and fortune and glory in my chosen field. So, we were off . . . right into the biggest blizzard of the century. It got so bad we couldn't see the horses in front of the wagon. Eventually our wagon hit a rut and went over an incline. We toppled over and Marjory, our baby, and her father were all killed. I buried them in the snow with my bare hands and rode out of there, bareback, on one of the horses. I wandered around for a few years picking up odd jobs, here and there, scratching in the dirt and such, and eventually discovered this place. I've found a little peace and quiet here."

"Maybe too peaceful, you think?" I suggested.

"Maybe," he replied shrugging sadly. "Maybe so."

I left it at that, and after a while went inside to catch some shut-eye. When I left him, Al was still smoking his pipe and quietly staring up at the stars.

Two days later, Al pronounced me almost ready to go. He lent me a felt slouch hat and a long overcoat. "It'll hide that fancy pistol of yours," he explained. "Anyone sees that fancy pearl-handled Colt, they'll recognize you right off. I'd recommend you reverse the pistol in the holster and slide the belt around so the gun rides the small of your back. Either that, or wear it like a shoulder holster around your neck. That way you can still reach the pistol, but it won't show when you walk around town."

"You mean when I limp around," I joked.

"Right. Now you're gettin' it. Just remember to roll your lips over your teeth to hide them and smack your lips once in a while. Gives some age to the part," he recommended.

I looked at my new friend. "I know you want to come with me, but I don't want you getting in the line of fire. No need to put yourself out that much. You've done enough."

"Hell, son, that's what friends are for. Besides, this is the most fun I've had since I left the stage. Gets mighty lonely just fishing and reading every day."

"All right. But, remember, if you do bump into me and there are any problems, don't put yourself at risk. I mean it, Al. Don't go all Davy Crockett on me."

"Don't worry about me. I'm not going to do anything foolish. Not in my nature. Truth be told, it wasn't really in Davy's nature, either. Tell you what, I'll give you plenty of time to wander around some, get some investigating done, and then I'll come in."

"You sure about this?" I asked. "Won't that be

a trifle suspicious? After all, you just got back from town."

"Stop worrying. Folks will think nothing of it. I go in for supplies regularly, and sometimes just for a drink or two or to mingle for a while. I've become kind of a fixture down there. It'll be fine," he said, grinning to reassure me.

The next afternoon I prepared to leave for town. Al had spent the better part of the morning checking my disguise one last time and giving me a little last minute coaching and planning. One problem I had to deal with was that my ankle wasn't in good enough shape to walk all the way to town on, and I didn't relish riding that far on Crackers. Given her size, riding that little burro would be worse than walking.

"I got it," Al said, after I voiced my concern. "I'll lend you my Grulla, Delilah. You can tie Crackers's lead rope to the saddle horn. They get along pretty well."

"But what'll you do, Al?" I asked. "If I've got your horse, you'll be stuck here. How will you get to town? Besides, somebody could recognize her?"

"That's easy enough," he replied. "Before you get to Blue Lake Ridge, take off Delilah's bridle, put it in the saddlebag, and slap her on the rump."

"She knows the way back that well?"

Al nodded his head. "Better'n I do. She'll come right back here."

One other thing bothered me. "You sure no one will recognize Crackers. I don't want to be arrested for horse theft, or donkey theft . . . or whatever."

"Don't worry about it, son," he replied. "Folks've only seen me in town on Delilah. You just let her loose before you get to town, and then walk the rest of the way in, leading Crackers, and you'll be fine."

I saddled the Grulla, put the crutch into the empty rifle scabbard, and walked her and the burro over to the cabin. Mounting up, I bid *adiós* to Al. He stood there and laughed at me.

"What is it?" I asked.

"You look like a character I played once. Grizzled old fellow named *Don* Quixote."

"I remember him," I answered. "My ma read me the story." Even I had to admit that sitting atop that old swayback with my old man disguise, wrinkled skin, and white hair, I must have looked like I had stepped right out of La Mancha. There was even a burro coming along to boot.

"All you need is a lance and you'd be all set."

I patted the crutch. "Got one. So you see, I may be tilting at a few windmills myself."

"*Adiós, companero.*"

I gave Delilah a nudge with my heel and waved one last good bye to my friend.

163

"Break a leg!" he shouted after me.

I rode off puzzled by his send-off. Why would he wish that on me after all my other aches and pains I wondered.

The ride to town was uneventful. Even though my trusty steed was hardly what that magazine of Al's would call swift-footed, she was easy going, sure, and surprisingly comfortable to ride. That was just fine with me since my ribs were still sore. I've always found the quiet solitude of the trail refreshing, and I finally managed to relax and enjoy the ride.

It seems to me, there comes a time during a ride when the rider and horse become as one. The *creaking* of the saddle and the rhythm of the rider begin to blend. Your mind sort of drifts back to good times as the horse's breathing starts to match yours. All becomes right with the world. A peaceful ride on horseback is my definition of paradise. I suppose I'm as God-fearing as the next fellow, but my church doesn't have a roof over it. When I want to discuss something with the Lord, I tend to do it on horseback, out in the open. I figure, that way, it stays between Him and me. Oh, I'm not saying I have all the answers, but wooden structures with latches on the doors don't do it for me. When I hear "Temple of the Lord," I tend to think in terms of tall trees, clouds, and distant mountain tops. But that's just me. I believe like my pa taught me. He always let other folks worship as they pleased and believed they should do the same for us.

We arrived at the far edge of town around dusk, which suited me fine. I hoped it would be a case of the less light the better, since I didn't truly know how realistic this disguise of mine looked to others. I only had Al's word to go by and prayed his eyesight was still good enough for the job.

I dismounted from Delilah and removed the crutch from the scabbard. I cross-tied her reins loosely over the saddle, pointed her in the right direction, and gave her a sound pat on the rump. She looked back at me as if to indicate her displeasure, and then trotted off back home.

"Well, Crackers," I said, turning to the little burro, "I guess it's just you and me now, so we might as well get started." Crackers looked back in the direction Delilah had taken and hesitated.

"I like it back there with old Al, too," I whispered to her. "Look, I'm not that all-fired excited about this trip, either, but we don't have a choice." I tucked the crutch under my arm to get into character, and, yanking on the rope, added: "There's no time like the present, Crackers, so don't give me a hard time." I probably meant the comment more for myself than the burro. "If we're gonna go, let's get going," I urged, tugging once more on her lead.

We entered the town about an hour later with

the sun almost down. I limped straight to the inn, determined to pass my first test quickly, and then hole up in my room. Remembering Al's advice, I smacked my gums, pulled my slouch hat down low over my face, and tied Crackers up at the hitching post. Her pack was light so she'd be fine there for the rest of the night. To get into character, I began mumbling to myself and limped through the door.

Millie was at the front desk, looking as cute as ever. The way I figured things, if she didn't recognize me or suspect anything out of the ordinary, then I had a fair-to-middling chance of carrying off this ruse. If she did suspect something, then I prayed she would give me the benefit of the doubt and listen to me before sounding the alarm. I had her pegged as the least likely in town to turn me in.

"Hello, young lady," I said, slowly approaching the desk. "Got a room for a tired old fool?"

Millie paused for a second before replying, and for that brief moment my heart rode up into my throat. "Don't see any old fools around here," she said, and smiled, "but gentlemen like yourself are welcome to sign here." She turned the hotel registry around and handed me a pen.

After a sigh of relief I smacked my gums and mumbled: "Gentleman. Heh, nobody ever called me that before." I started to sign my name and got to the W in William before catching myself

166

and writing "Walters," instead. I kept my head lowered the whole time and hunkered down over the book to avoid catching her eye. When Millie began reaching for a key, I pointed to the one for the room I had stayed in during my previous stay, saying: "How about that one, missy? That's my lucky number, see, and I really don't want to climb too many stairs. These ol' legs just aren't what they used to be. It's the rheumatism, I guess."

"Certainly, Mister Walters. No problem at all. Here you go," she replied, handing me the key. "Do you need any help with your bags?"

I shook my head. "Not much to carry 'cepting these old bones, but I'm much obliged, anyway." I turned away quickly and, mumbling gibberish to myself, climbed the stairs up to my room.

CHAPTER FOURTEEN

Once inside my room, I collapsed with my back against the door. I was quickly finding this game a most nerve-racking ordeal. I'd been in towns where mob rule occurred, and it wasn't pleasant. I knew if anyone were to point me out to the sheriff, there would be an immediate necktie party with my neck as the invited guest. My only option would have been to shoot my way out of town, and I didn't relish harming innocent people.

While I hadn't met all that many folks during my last visit to Blue Lake Ridge, I knew that, in a town this small, word travels fast. I didn't know who the gang was that had robbed the bank, where they were now, or even if they were still in town, but, somehow or another, I had to figure it all out and then find them in order to clear my name.

While leaning against the door, I looked up and remembered why I'd selected this particular room. I made sure the door was locked, and then pulled a chair over and climbed up to check the hidey-hole I'd made in that ceiling panel.

When I pulled the pair of saddlebags down, I breathed a big sigh of relief. When she had asked for help, Judy didn't know I had any money, but I suspected from the tone of her letter that she desperately needed it. I was willing to do anything for Sis, including risking my life, but that didn't mean I wanted to recklessly throw it away. So the question now was how to get the money safely and quickly to her while at the same time staying out of danger. Even if I managed to keep this disguise going, the minute I mentioned my name at the bank, I'd be a dead man. At the very least they'd confiscate my gold. As it was, I was worried. I'd lost too much time already, and time was one thing my sister and her husband Andy could ill afford.

Sitting on the bed, the realization hit me that my name needn't even come up. I actually slapped my forehead when I realized how simple it could be, and what a lame brain I was for not thinking this out earlier. Here I was fretting all this time about getting money sent to my sister from a town where everyone despised me as a low-down bank robber, when, all along, I should have remembered that Judith's last name had changed from Grayson to Maguire when she married. Not only that, but I was now disguised as an old prospector known simply as Mr. Walters. All I had to do was head to the bank, change the gold to currency, and arrange to have it sent east to the Maguire family. My real name need never come up. That night, I went to bed safe in my room with my saddlebags tucked under one arm, and my Navy Colt under the other. I slept like a baby.

I awoke bright and early the next morning and spent a half hour at the mirror re-applying the make-up and hair Al had given me. I truly do not understand how fancy women do this day after day, but I swear, as God is my witness, that I will never again fuss at one for being late. That damned mirror had me convinced that I had made a botched job of it. Fortunately Al explained to me that nobody looks directly at you for very long, or examines your face all that closely unless they want to kiss or punch you in the face. Since it was a sure bet nobody was going to kiss the old puss I saw reflected back at me in the mirror, I resolved to get on with it, and headed downstairs to the lobby.

I was almost out the front door before I stopped and turned around, remembering something very important. I went back into the lobby and over to the refreshment table and grabbed a couple of those doughnuts I had tried the last time I was in town. That was one opportunity I just couldn't pass up. Using my crutch to push open the front door, I chuckled to myself as I went out into the street with powdered sugar leaving a trail behind and on me.

I unhitched Crackers and walked her down the street. The bank was four blocks south of the inn

170

and one block down the street on the lakeshore side of town. Once I got there, I tied her up, took a feedbag off the pack, and put it over the burro's head. I walked, or I should say hobbled, up to the front door, preparing to enter the bank when a large poster made me pause. Nailed to the wall next to the door was a full size sketch of me right under the words Wanted Dead or Alive. They were very big letters, indeed, but what was more interesting was that someone had scribbled But Dead is Better! right across the poster. Clearly the local townsfolk weren't in the mood to consider the possibility of other explanations to the robbery where it concerned me. I blew out a small sigh, making sure my slouch hat was pulled down low, and limped into the bank.

I found the bank's layout to be fairly typical. Its lobby formed a large square, in the middle of which stood a tall double-sided desk that was waist height and sloped downward, making it easier for clients to fill out bank forms and such while still standing. Off to the right was a row of tellers who were separated from the customers by a series of windows picketed with bars. Money was interchanged through small slots. Behind the tellers, I could see two doors, one that led to the bank president's office and another that I assumed led to the vault. It seemed a fairly secure arrangement.

I looked for signs of forced entry, but all the windows had bars on them, and they appeared intact. When I had entered the front door, it had shown no signs of damage, either. I supposed it could have been repaired during the time I had been gone, but I highly doubted that the robbers had gained entry through the only door that faced the street. Even at night, that would have been much too risky. I quickly glanced around, and it was then that I noticed a large hole in the wall, near the floor, next to the president's office. It had been temporarily patched with large metal plates bolted down over the hole. Now I knew where the gang had entered.

Remembering to keep my head down and continuing to limp, I approached a mousy-looking receptionist. She looked up and nodded. "My name is Miss Prescott . . . may I help you?" From the way she had emphasized "miss," I had her pegged as a spinster. She appeared to be in her mid-forties and had a rather pale complexion. She was thin as a rail and wore a pair of those little spectacles with the chain that goes behind the neck. I figured she needed it to catch them from falling off her pencil-thin nose.

Perhaps I was being a trifle hard on her, but bank folks weren't real high on my list right then. For one thing, the bank back home was foreclosing on my brother-in-law without cutting him any slack, and now this bank's inability to

172

protect the town's savings had put me in my present predicament.

"Got anyone around here who can change some gold for me, and then send it on to someone else without it gettin' lost?" I asked.

Miss Prescott's expression told me she wasn't amused by how I had phrased my question.

"Mister Tidewell will be right with you," she replied curtly.

I put my hand to my ear, feigning deafness. "Eh? How's that, missy? What bides well?"

"No, it's Mister Tidewell," she replied, frustrated. "He's one of four assistant managers."

I stared at her.

"Just wait here a moment," she added, shaking her head. She then went over to one of the other desks behind hers, whispering something to the man seated there.

The man looked up at me, nodded, and then stood and approached me. He was wearing one of those Sunday-go-to-meeting navy blue suits with all the buttons and a vest complete with gold chain and pocket watch. His shoes were the lace-up kind and were polished enough to give back a reflection. He also wore spectacles but they were the kind without any ear-pieces. I figured he chose that kind so he could play with them, nervously pushing them up and down his nose while turning down loans for widows and orphans.

"Cornelius Tidewell at your service, sir," he said loudly. "Miss Prescott mentioned something about changing some gold for you?"

"That's right, sonny, and it's a fair sum. Got some place we can talk?" I asked, using my best old-timer's voice.

"Certainly. Right over here at my desk. Please have a seat, Mister . . . ?"

"Walters. New to town and want to change some glitter." I made sure to let my crutch fall against his highly polished desk as I sat down. I remembered Al's admonition about disguising yourself. *Distraction, distraction, distraction.*

Sure enough, instead of paying attention to my face, Mr. Cornelius Tidewell took a rag from one of the desk drawers and quickly polished the corner where the crutch had struck. He then cleaned his glasses before addressing me further. Finally: "Normally we would refer you to the assayer's office for the gold conversion," he explained, "and then ask you to return, but at present that office is closed."

"Still?" I blurted out.

"How's that?" he asked.

"*Er* . . . I meant I'd rather do all that here if it's possible. Walkin' ain't easy for me. . . ."

"I'm afraid we have no other choice," cut in Mr. Tidewell. "It seems the assayer is sitting in jail," he explained.

"Really?"

"Yes, you see there was an altercation at the assayer's a while back after which the assayer accompanied the sheriff to his office. Our sheriff apparently discovered an old poster indicating that he was wanted in several states for various other crimes, such as fraud and embezzlement. He's been sitting in our jail ever since, waiting for the circuit judge to arrive."

"Ain't that somethin'," I said, chuckling to myself. Obviously I could eliminate the assayer as a prime suspect if he had spent the whole time in jail. Unfortunately, while that little tidbit of news eliminated one suspect from my list, it didn't add any new ones in its place.

"Now then, Miss Prescott will take your gold and have it analyzed. It may take just a little longer, but we can use the time to fill out the forms to help you open an account."

"Nope, no accounts fer me. I want to send it all to my si— . . . um . . . granddaughter. Can't you do one of them money things?" I asked.

"Yes, I suppose so." His eyes wandered over to one of several wanted posters of me that hung on the walls of the bank.

I dropped my saddlebags heavily on his desk, which succeeded in knocking over my crutch again. As expected, it brought his attention back to his desk.

Cornelius gestured to Miss Prescott, who promptly picked the bags up and left with the gold.

"Now then . . . where do you want this sent?" he asked, leaning over and polishing his desk again.

I handed him a slip of paper with my sister's address, as well as that of the Saving's and Trust. "Can you get this there *pronto*?" I inquired.

"If it is in a location within reason," he replied. "We shall see. One moment please." He arose and went to a small side table and began thumbing through a large ledger of sorts. He returned and sat back down, saying: "It will be no trouble at all. We should be able to get it there within two weeks, or so. If we can't telegraph it, we can use a registered Wells Fargo delivery service."

"Safe?" I asked.

"I can guarantee safe delivery of any funds entrusted to us," he declared proudly.

"That so? It's just that I heard this here bank went and got itself robbed a while back. Was that money guaranteed, too?"

Tidewell seemed rather annoyed. "Well, that hardly was our fault. The robber struck at night, during a holiday celebration."

"So how'd he get in if you're so all fired safe and guaranteed?" I asked rudely.

"He blew a hole in the wall back there," he replied.

"And nobody heard a wall gettin' blowed up?" I asked.

"That wall faces a vacant lot. Apparently he

176

came in under cover of darkness and timed the explosion to coincide with the fireworks display we were having. Seems he was a stranger by the name of Grayson who was completely unknown in these parts." He paused to point at one of the Wanted posters. "Made a clean getaway."

"How'd a stranger know when them fireworks would go off?" I wondered aloud.

"I'm sure I don't know," Cornelius answered abruptly. "Maybe he asked around."

It seemed nobody in this town was giving the robbery the slightest afterthought. Stranger comes to town, stranger robs bank, stranger makes clean getaway. It explained everything perfectly. Problem was I knew it wasn't true, but couldn't prove it to anyone without getting shot or hung first, especially if everyone else in town had Tidewell's profound sense of curiosity.

"But don't worry," he added. "We now have a man, day and night, to protect our bank."

"Locking the barn door after the horse is gone, eh?" I cackled.

He coughed and readjusted his glasses. "We have another rather large bank in Denver, which of course is how we managed to stay in business, even after the robbery. Your transaction will be well protected, I assure you."

Miss Prescott finally returned with a slip of paper.

Cornelius Tidewell's eyes dilated when he read

the amount. "My goodness, this is a substantial amount, Mister Walters." He started staring at me in disbelief, impressed at the fortune I had been carrying around in a pair of old saddlebags.

"By crackity, it is that," I said, thumping his desk with the top of my crutch. "Done found me a glory hole!"

"How's that?" he asked, becoming more perturbed at the damage my crutch was doing to his desk's finish.

"Go figure it," I explained. "All them years of grubbing around for nothin', and then one night I'm just sleeping near an old dig and lightning goes and strikes this tree."

Both Cornelius and his secretary seemed fascinated. I hoped they'd concentrate more on the story than on my face. "The next morning, my burro is grazing around them tree roots and when I go to fetch her, there it is. A glory hole." I could see the banker's eyes light up, so I quickly put out the fire. "But don't go gettin' your hopes up, 'cause there ain't no more, not that I'd tell you iffen there were."

"How can you be sure?" he asked.

"I looked all around them parts for two more weeks, but this was all there was. Like I said, a glory hole."

"Very well. If you will just sign this, Miss Prescott will get the process started. Would you like to include a message with it?"

"Just say it's from W.G.," I replied, without thinking.

Mr. Tidewell looked puzzled. "W.G.? What's the G for, if I might ask?"

"*Er . . .* ," I stumbled. "It's my middle name . . . Wendell Gregory Walters. Si— . . . m-my granddaughter will know who it's from. She calls me W.G. for short." I felt the walls beginning to close in on me and decided it was time to end this little visit. I was happy about one thing though— the money was finally on its way to Judith. I'd sworn to Pa I'd watch out for her, and, regardless of whatever else might happen to me, I'd kept my promise. Besides, I now had more information about the robbery, and anything that might help keep me out of a hangman's noose or a pine box was important as far as I was concerned.

I got up from my chair and pulled my hat down a little lower. Then after saying good bye and making sure to fumble my crutch against the desk, I hobbled slowly out the door.

Distraction. Distraction. Distraction.

CHAPTER FIFTEEN

After leaving the bank, I paused for a moment. I looked up and down the street trying to decide which way to jump. Getting Judith's money taken care of at the bank was a load off my mind, but it didn't bring me any closer to finding out who the gang members were.

I walked over to the little burro, and, as I was untying her, I noticed the window of Frederick's Mercantile and Hardware Store across the street. Written on the window underneath an advertisement for Wire, Nails, Nuts, and Bolts was a large drawing of a sunburst with the words Explosive Sale printed inside the drawing.

"Must have prices that will blow you away," I mumbled to the burro. Crackers looked up at me like I was crazy. It was then that I got to thinking about explosives. When that gang blew a hole in the bank, they had to have been using dynamite, and maybe, just maybe, they bought it here in town. It wasn't much to go on, but it was all I had at the time. I figured it couldn't hurt to check out Frederick's. Besides, who knows when you might find a bargain? I walked Crackers over to the mercantile and tied her up again. "You wait here," I whispered in her ear. "I'll see if they have any sugar cubes."

I was impressed by the size of the store. There were three rows of shelving with assorted canned goods, and both walls were lined with hat racks, more shelves with clothing, bolts of linen, and miscellaneous household supplies. There was a pharmacy in back with rows of jars containing assorted pills and powders, and there was a section for the children with candy sticks, jaw-breakers, and lollipops. Off to the right side was a small area with two square tables, around which the older men apparently gathered to play checkers and to discuss the events of the day. The way the conversation was going, it was little wonder Al found it so easy to pick up information.

"Howdy," I said to the group as I entered.

Two of the men looked up from the checker-board and nodded. For a moment, I worried that one of the older men had noticed something odd about my get-up or the make-up, but he immediately returned to the game, obviously considering that more important than a lame old prospector.

I hobbled through the store until a middle-aged man in a white apron greeted me.

"Something I can help you find, mister?" he asked.

"Well, I'm a lookin' fer a few things," I replied. "Don't expect as I'll be a-needing them right off, but I wanted to see iffen I could stock up later, when I'm ready to leave town."

"Well, we have quite an assortment of supplies. I expect we can accommodate you," he boasted.

I glanced at the shelves. "I reckon so. Gonna need some sugar cubes for my burro for one thing."

He laughed. "No problem with that. Here you go," he said, pulling the top from one of the glass jars. I took a handful. "What else?"

I made a show of looking around the shop until I dropped the question I had come in for. "Got any dynamite? Figure on doing me a little prospecting."

"At your age?" he laughed.

"Sure am, and watch your mouth. You're gonna be my age soon enough, and, when you are, just remember there's no use complainin' about gettin' old, 'cause the only other alternative is much worse."

He cleared his throat. "Sorry about that. And the answer is yes. We keep a fair supply of it."

"Lots o' other prospectors buy here, do they?" I inquired.

"Well, there are some, but mostly we sell it to ranchers in the area," he answered.

"That so? What'd ranchers need it fer?"

"Well, let's see . . . some use it for blowing tree stumps to clear the land, some use it to dig a well, and a couple of scoundrels use it to fish with," he explained.

"Fish with?" I asked, puzzled.

"Sure. If you're too lazy to wait on the fish, you just chuck in a stick and wait for the explosion to bring them up. Then you net the fish and head for home and the frying pan."

"Don't quite seem fair to me," I commented.

"Ain't. But it is quick," he said, with a smile. "Right, Charley? You ought to know."

One of the men at the checkers table waved his arm. "*Ah,* go blow it out your arse, Frederick."

The shopkeeper just laughed at him. "Don't worry," he said, turning back to me. "We'll fill your needs, whatever they may be. I pride myself on keeping a good stock level of the necessities."

"Good, 'cause I reckon I'll be needing some grub and a shovel or two when I get set to leave," I remarked.

"Any idea when that'll be?" he inquired.

"Oh, it'll probably be a couple of days from now I expect. Town livin's a bit frisky for my taste. Folks is always in a hurry fer one thing, and towns always seem a mite rowdy fer my taste."

The shopkeeper laughed. "Think so?"

"Sure," I replied. "Fer instance, didn't you folks go an' get your bank robbed a while back?"

"I see your point," he replied. "Yes, as a matter of fact we did."

"Blowed a big hole in the bank I heard."

"That's right. Happened during the holiday fireworks display we had here," he remarked.

"Too bad. Say, you reckon they used dynamite

for that job?" I asked, scratching the top of my head.

"Well, if they did, they didn't get it from us," Mr. Frederick replied curtly.

"None missing, huh?"

"Not a stick!" he replied.

"How's come you're so sure?" I asked.

"Because our sheriff checked on that right after the robbery. Thought maybe this Grayson fellow, the one who robbed the place, had also broken in here. Since nothing was missing and Grayson didn't purchase any here, Sheriff Kent figured that he must have brought a couple of sticks with him when he rode into town. The liveryman said he had a couple of big saddlebags with him when he rode in."

"Maybe he stole it from one of them ranchers or fishermen fellows you was talking about," I remarked.

"Doesn't appear that way. Nobody reported any missing. And trust me, out here folks would notice something like that," he explained.

"Guess so." I was running out of questions and didn't want to push my luck by appearing too inquisitive.

"Well, thanks, sonny." I reached into my pocket for some change. "I'll just take this sugar for my burro and be a-going fer now. How much I owe you?"

"Keep your change. You just come back here to

buy your supplies and the sugar's on the house," he said.

"Mighty neighborly of you," I said. "I'll be a-thankin' you kindly. Good day to you."

"See you later," he replied as I limped out the door.

I had pushed my luck enough for one day. Al had mentioned that this type of stage make-up tended to break down and run after a while. I wasn't quite sure how long a while was, but I wasn't going to take any chances. Before leaving for town, I had asked Al to be more specific, but he explained that it varied according to conditions. "Some stages are real hot, what with being indoors and having a lot of lights on you. Other times, you might be acting outdoors and it'd be real cool, like at a fair or carnival or such. I expect this make-up should last you a while. But it depends."

I untied Crackers and returned to the inn. I tied her to the rail outside and put on her feedbag. I was getting fond of the little burro and gave her a pat on her rump. That's when she kicked me right in the shin of my bad leg. Crutch or no crutch, I entered the inn limping even more this time. I went straight through the lobby to my room and bolted the door.

I took off my overcoat, undid the holster from around my shoulder, and tossed them on the bed. I washed the make-up off in the basin that was next to the bed, and, after drying off, I dropped down into a large armchair next to the window. I pulled the curtain over the window in case anyone might glance up and get curious. There was no sense in taking unnecessary chances. I was taking enough necessary ones as it was.

On the side table next to the chair, someone had placed a copy of the *Daily Advocate*. I hadn't paid much attention, during my previous stay, but it was obvious that Millie had put it there. There was also a peppermint sitting on the bed's pillow. *Nice touch,* I thought as I picked up the paper and read through the usual local stories. There was an article about the importance of trying to attract the railroad to the area, and another about how much the price of farm produce had risen since the last election. I laughed aloud when I read a political commentary that stated: *If you're not a Democrat by the time you're eighteen, you have no heart. If you're not a Republican by the time you are thirty, you have no brain.*

Sounds like something my uncle Jake would have written, I thought.

There was a nice short story on page three about an express rider who had barely escaped from a band of renegade Indians by jumping his horse over a wide gully. The Indians apparently had never learned to jump their horses that far. It was poppycock, but made for a good read. Finally I

186

turned the page and read a small paragraph at the bottom of the left side entitled, *Bank Robber Still at Large.* I read on.

> Sheriff Kent reports that apparently there are no further clues to pursue regarding the whereabouts of the notorious bank robber, William Grayson. The full details of the robbery of the Blue Lake Ridge Bank, as reported in the last issue of the *Advocate,* are by now well known about town. . . .

I should read that issue, I thought as I drifted off to sleep, still sitting up in the armchair.

I woke up some hours later, woozy, with a stiff neck, a sore shin, and a hungry stomach. I draped a large towel over my head in case someone were to see me, and, making sure the coast was clear, hurried to the privy. When I got back, I again bolted the door and sat down in front of the mirror to re-apply the grease paint, something I was fast learning to dislike. I had no choice, however, as my stomach was beginning to take over from my brain. Once the mirror had me convinced that I could pass muster, I headed downstairs for dinner.

I chose a table in the far corner of the inn's dining room. When the waitress, an elderly lady named Irma, came to my table, I remained hidden behind my menu. It was rather rude to order that way, but much safer. I started out with lima bean soup and proceeded through a plate of buffalo steak with cheese potatoes—a dinner that was extraordinarily good. Even though I kept myself inconspicuous while eating, I did manage to eye the others in the room. I didn't really expect anyone to leap up and confess, but, still, you never know when someone might let something slip, especially after a full stomach and couple of brews. Unfortunately the room was as quiet as a husband at his wife's Wednesday night sewing circle. I finished dinner with a double helping of peach cobbler, a dessert, which as promised, did live up to its reputation, and then returned to my room, disappointed but stuffed to the gills.

Before hitting the sack, I retrieved the spare cylinder for my Colt, which I always carried in a leather pouch, and resealed the cylinder bores. It was a trick my pa had taught me when I was younger. Even with as fine a weapon as the Colt, a freak powder flash will sometimes ignite the rest of the powder in the other cylinder chambers. Sealing them with beeswax or tallow helps prevent a multiple misfire and can save your hand for future use.

The spare cylinder was my uncle Jake's idea. He explained that, while some lawmen carry a second pistol, those shootists, wishing to keep things simple, carry just a second but fully loaded cylinder. It is almost faster to get back into action and a heck of a lot lighter to carry around all day than a second gun and holster. Whenever possible, I also liked to fire the chambers out every day and then reload the pistol. It was a mite expensive and time consuming, but was safer and insured a clean blast each and every time. Obviously I couldn't do that in my present surroundings without attracting attention, so a good cleaning and oiling would have to suffice.

When I was finished, I propped the chair under the doorknob for further security and went to bed to mull the day's events over. I didn't get much mulling done, and before long was fast asleep.

The next morning, after what was becoming a tiresome routine in front of the mirror, I left the inn. The little burro was still tied up in front of the hotel, so I removed her hobbles and refilled her feedbag with some oats from her pack. I then walked her over to the office of the *Advocate* and left her tied up in front, munching contentedly while I went inside.

The place was fair sized and smelled of cleaning solutions and freshly cut paper. There was a short wooden rail with a swinging half door dividing the lobby from the work area and the editor's desk. I noticed a framed newspaper hanging on the wall near the doorway and stopped to read it. It was a first issue copy of the *Advocate* and a picture of Millie's father, the paper's founder. I couldn't help but notice the family resemblance. There was a steam-operated printing press off to the right where a young workman was busy tightening a bolt with a large wrench.

"Good morning, sir, may I help you?" a voice said from behind me.

I recognized the owner at once. "Oh, yes, thank you. How are you, Mister Ellsworth?"

The newspaperman stared at me curiously. "I'm sorry . . . do I know you?" he asked.

Suddenly the room became much smaller and a lot warmer. Just as Al had warned I had gotten distracted and forgotten my place. Falling out of character, I believe he called it. I glanced around in desperation till my eyes caught hold of his desk.

"*Er* . . . Why . . . no, sir. Just assumed that's your name. That is your nameplate over thar on the desk, ain't it?" I pointed.

He looked over to the desk. "Why, yes. How very observant of you," he remarked.

"Got to notice things when you're out prospectin'. Different rocks and such," I explained.

Ellsworth chuckled and motioned me over to a chair. "Makes sense, of course. Please, make yourself comfortable. Now then, what is it we can do for you?"

"Got any back issues of this here paper I can look at?" I inquired.

"Well, yes, we do keep a back archive. May

I ask what specifically you are looking for?"

What indeed? I began to sweat a bit. Foolishly I hadn't thought things through all that well and was about to stick my foot even farther down my mouth if I didn't think fast.

"Well, sir, it's like this. At my age, I found that grubbin' around in the dirt ain't the only way to find clues when you're prospecting fer glitter. Thought maybe I'd see iffen there weren't something in this here newspaper of your'n about recent strikes. Also, I heerd you all went and got your bank robbed and I don't want to wander around uninformed with a robber on the loose."

"I should hope not," he replied, getting up from his chair. "Here let me show you to the stack of back issues."

I tipped my hat. "Much obliged." I felt Al would have been proud of my performance.

I followed Mr. Ellsworth to the back of the office where he pointed to a long table located against the far wall. On the table were several large, leather bound books, each labeled with dates representing previous months.

"I'm sure you will find all the information on local goings on in these," Mr. Ellsworth proudly boasted. "If you want to start with the information on the robbery, I suggest you look in the August edition." He pointed to one of the books. "It happened between the night

191

of the fourteenth and the fifteenth, if I recall correctly."

"Mind if I pull up a chair?" I asked.

"Not a problem, just call if you need me."

Once he returned to his work, I thumbed through the August ledger until I found what I was looking for. There in big headlines was the whole story.

Town Bank Robbed
During Holiday Celebration
Sheriff Kent Investigates

When the folks of our lovely community awoke yesterday, most were still recovering from the gaiety and reverie that took place the night before, during our Founder's Day Celebration. It wasn't until the next morning, when the director of our bank, Mr. Franklin Harris, and his assistant, Mr. Cornelius Tidewell, opened the front door, that they noticed a rather sizeable hole across the lobby in the back wall. Fearing the worst, they rushed to the vault where they immediately found the door to the safe was ajar.

Someone had blown a hole in the rear wall of the bank, apparently with dynamite. Once inside, they had then drilled the lock mechanism and apparently poured some sort of acid into the hole in order to force the vault open. "It was a very skilled robbery, if you ask me," Mr. Harris is quoted as saying.

When asked about the sum that was stolen, Cornelius Tidewell, assistant manager, had this to add: "We are still calculating the accounts and losses, but obviously it was substantial. I'm afraid it was a terrible blow to our clientele. Even so, I can assure you we continue to strive to better protect our patrons' savings to the utmost. This is devastating to all of us, but whoever is responsible will pay, I assure you. I'm sure the bank will be offering a reward for the blaggard who perpetrated this dastardly deed."

Sheriff Kent was immediately informed of the robbery and began his investigation at once. Within short order, he ascertained that none of the town's regular inhabitants were missing. Furthermore, since no one was aware that there had been a break-in, Kent reasoned that the fireworks must have covered the sound of the dynamite.

One suspect stands out, however. "There was this rather troublesome sort hanging around town. On at least two occasions he was involved in violent acts, such as fisticuffs or gunplay," Kent is reported as saying. "His name, if it's not an alias, is William Grayson. Not surprisingly both he and his horse are missing."

Several of our townsfolk reported witnessing the above mentioned acts of violence perpetrated by this low-life. Even more condemning was the testimony of the rather charming Mrs. June Elliott, a widow who is new to our community. When questioned by our reporter, she mentioned that Grayson had offered to escort her to the livery that evening, but then mysteriously disappeared around the same time as the break-in is believed to have occurred. Upon checking the livery, Sheriff Kent was not surprised to learn that the proprietor, Mr. Mike Turner, had seen Grayson ride hurriedly out of town late that night. According to his description the man's saddlebags appeared stuffed to capacity.

I turned to the next page.

Sheriff Kent is organizing a posse to hunt down the only known suspect in the bank robbery, William Grayson. By all accounts, he is described as being in his early to mid-twenties, standing about six foot three or four and weighing around one hundred eighty to two hundred pounds. Grayson wears a big handlebar moustache and carries a rather large Bowie knife. Most who saw him in town mentioned that he also carries a rather impressive pearl-handled Navy Colt pistol, apparently silver- or nickel-plated. Mr. Turner reported he rode out of town on a large palomino stallion. Men between the ages of sixteen and sixty are encouraged to report to the sheriff's office no later than 1:00 p.m. this afternoon. Bring your own rifle and horse and supplies for a five-day ride. There will be a moderate daily wage for anyone participating in the posse, plus a percentage of any reward that the bank might offer, should the money be recovered.

The article then went on to add:

Of note is this official proclamation from the Sheriff's Office.
DUE TO THE SEVERITY OF THE CRIME TO OUR PEACEFUL TOWN, POSSE MEMBERS ARE INSTRUCTED TO SHOOT FIRST AND ASK QUESTIONS LATER. DEAD OR ALIVE IS THE ORDER OF THE DAY.

Low-life indeed, I thought angrily. There really wasn't much in the report that I could use to clear my name. Quite the contrary, it amazed me at how little it took to condemn a man in this town. Even if it were true, simply riding out of town with full saddlebags didn't merit a Dead or Alive order. I guess they never heard of a fair trial in this county. I shook my head and, as I rose from the table, I made sure my pistol was still well concealed up under my slicker.

"Find anything of interest?" Mr. Ellsworth asked as I walked by.

"Seems like a real law and order sort of town from what I read," I replied.

"We do respect the peace in our little community," he agreed, nodding.

"Shoot first and ask questions later," I mumbled to myself angrily.

"How's that? Sorry, didn't quite hear you," he said.

"I said if I have any more questions later, I'll sure ask," I replied, exiting the office.

"Enjoy your stay in Blue Lake Ridge!" he called after me.

I waved back over my shoulder. *I should live so long,* I thought to myself.

CHAPTER SIXTEEN

It was definitely time for a good stiff drink. I was fairly confident that I could remain unrecognized, so naturally I made straight for the saloon, Crackers again in tow. As I approached the batwing doors, I noticed a Pawnee Indian standing next to the doorway. He had a shaved head with a thin strip of hair down the middle in what back home we called a Mohawk. He had on buckskin pants with fringes on them, a bear-claw necklace, and a long, folded red blanket that he wore diagonally across his shoulder. It wasn't necessarily unusual to see friendly Indians in a Western town but a Pawnee in this neck of the woods seemed a bit out of their usual stomping grounds. He seemed harmless enough and the local folks walking by only gave him the occasional glance.

I don't speak that particular tribe's lingo, but I do know some plains sign language, so I gave him the gesture most often used for greeting. I was a bit surprised that he didn't respond to my sign, but I figured he wasn't all that interested. He seemed to be avoiding eye contact with any of the whites who passed him by so I just shrugged my shoulders, pushed the doors open, and went on in.

I chose a table in the back of the room. It stood to reason the closer I was to the door, the better chance I might have for a getaway, in case I was recognized. While pulling up a chair, I couldn't help but notice another one of those Wanted posters of me tacked to the wall behind the table. This one had a bullet hole between the eyes. I swung the chair around and put my back to the wall, blocking the picture.

I thought it odd that the tables in the saloon had been rearranged and now there were colored paper lanterns hanging all around the room. There was also a whole stack of recently cut wildflowers bunched up in a heap in one corner, and a number of glass pitchers were stacked at the end of the bar near the flowers.

Behind the bartender the mirror had large letters painted over the glass that spelled out CONGRATULATIONS. I also noticed that the picture of a half naked lady had been turned around, with the picture side to the wall. The room was fairly full, and I recognized several faces from my first trip to town, including that of the reverend. I was a little surprised he was still in town. I'd have thought a traveling preacher would have moved on by now.

A young waiter came over and asked what I'd have. I kept my head lowered and began smacking my lips. "A beer'd be nice, sonny."

"Old-timer, if all you wanted was a drink you

could have gone to the bar. No need to take up a table."

I rapped my crutch against the table and shook my head. "No respect for the elderly any more," I mumbled. "I can't stand too long, see? It hurts my joints . . . what with the rheumatism and all. You young ones don't understand such things. Iffen you gotta bring something else, how about a bowl o' them bar nuts I see over there?"

"Big spender," he replied snidely. "Be right back."

He was a wise ass, but, when he returned, I tossed him a few extra coins, and all of a sudden his attitude changed for the better. When he turned to leave, I grabbed his wrist.

"One quick question, sonny. What's with all them girlie decorations you got all around the place?" I asked.

"Why they're for the wedding ceremony and the going-away party the town's throwing for the couple afterwards," he replied, surprised at the question.

"Someone getting hitched, is they?" I asked.

"I thought everyone knew about it. You must be new to town, huh? See, our local sheriff is getting married."

"No fooling. Someone snagged the law." I chuckled. "Who's he marryin' . . . the school-marm? No, let me guess, one of them cute saloon girls?"

"Quite the opposite. This lady's from out of town. Somewhere back east, I believe. She's a real gentle sort and quite a looker. Everyone says he's a real lucky feller."

Al had explained that, as soon as I was out of the picture, Mrs. Elliott and the sheriff had quickly become an item. I figured him for a fast operator with the ladies, but I didn't realize how much so, or how serious he'd become in so short a time. I'll admit to some jealousy, but, in my defense, I honestly did hope he'd treat her like she deserved and would make her happy.

"So how's come they's a-gettin' married here in the saloon? I thought I passed a church on the way into town?" I said.

"Oh, we got one, all right, but they both insisted on a civil ceremony," he explained. "Some folks is funny that way, I guess. Our town mayor's all puffed up over it. You know what I mean . . . real excited that they chose him to be the one performing the service. Won't stop bragging on it."

"He's doing the hitchin'? Not the reverend over there?" I asked.

"That's right . . . the mayor is," he said, lowering his voice a little. "You know the type. Any excuse for attention or any chance to make a speech gets him all worked up."

I nodded and laughed at his description. "You

mentioned a goin'-away party. You mean just fer their honeymoon?" I asked.

"Nope, most of us wish it were so," he began. "No, they're going away for good. Best sheriff we've had around here, too. Except for that one bank robbery, Sheriff Kent kept the place real safe and peaceful-like. Real popular around these parts. Even caught a crooked assayer a while back that nobody else suspected. The whole town's turning out for him."

"Nobody else suspected the assayer, eh?" I replied, shaking my head angrily. "Well, iffen the sheriff is so dang popular, how come he's leavin'?" I asked.

" 'Cause of the lady. I guess she's just not cut out to be the Western type. Never stops complaining about how hard it is out here, or how her first husband never would have died if he'd stayed back east. Heard tell she's got the sheriff so lovesick he can't see straight. Wants to make her happy, so he's moving back to the Carolinas with her."

I could tell the waiter was getting impatient.

"Listen, old-timer, thanks for the tip, but I got other tables to wait," he said, excusing himself.

After he left, I finished my beer and had another. I might have left the saloon after that first drink, but they had over-salted the nuts and now I was still thirsty. Besides, the piano player in the corner was playing "Greensleeves," and I was always a mite partial to that tune. Plus, the lady singer, who was sitting on the top of the piano, wasn't half bad to look at, especially for an old man like me.

I was beginning to feel the effects of the next few drinks when I overheard three men at the next table talking about the robbery. It brought me out of the haze.

"I know what everyone else in town says, but I still say it don't make sense," the skinnier of the three commented. "I heard from Bull that this Grayson fellow was in the assayer's office changing gold with him before the robbery. Why would someone with all that gold go and rob a bank?" he asked.

I would have bought that fellow a beer if I could have, but instead I just pulled my hat lower and scooted my chair closer. Good old Martin Turnbull. At least someone in town had stopped to think things through. Maybe these were the friends he'd mentioned.

"Are you kidding, Pete? Where do you suppose he got that gold in the first place? He probably stole it, too." It was the fat man, sitting opposite his friend, who made this comment.

He wouldn't get any beer from me, that's for sure, I thought angrily.

"Yeah, Joe's right," the third man said, putting in his two cents' worth. "Besides, Bull said he never actually saw any gold. Maybe this Grayson fellow was just scouting the place for another robbery."

I shook my head. My bar tab was decreasing by the moment. I'd heard enough. Even if there were a few men of common sense left in this town, the rest of the population would never consider listening to an alternative explanation for the robbery. Like they say, if you tell a lie about something enough times, it eventually becomes the truth. The only way I was getting out of this mess was to bring the gang to justice myself and to recover the gold. I figured if I could manage that little feat, I might just go to work solving some other simple problems, like ending poverty in the world or solving the riddle of the Sphinx.

I picked up my crutch, made a show of struggling to my feet, and hobbled out through the doors, mumbling to myself the whole time. And not all of my grumbling was an act, either.

I knew for sure where I was going next because of something the livery man had said to the sheriff. According to what Al had told me back at his cabin, and which I'd later confirmed by reading the *Advocate*, Mike Turner had claimed the robber barreled out of town without paying his livery bill, and supposedly had what looked like heavy, over-stuffed bags thrown over his saddle. There was no way that bum, Turner, at the stable could have mistaken someone else for me so soon after our first encounter, even at night.

That so, why would Turner lie about me, unless it was done in order to divert suspicion over to me? Since he was obviously trying to make me look guilty, it stood to reason that he must somehow be involved in the robbery.

I wasn't quite sure what his role was in all this, but my first impression was that Mike Turner wasn't anywhere near smart enough to pull off this kind of theft. He was more the type to ride up as part of another's gang, shoot first, and ask questions later. This robbery was more cleverly planned than that, pulled off during the dark of night without alerting a soul. Someone had robbed the town bank during a major holiday in order to cover their activities and to get an extra day's lead before the townsfolk knew what hit them. Then whoever it was went and blamed it on me.

Was Turner smart enough for that kind of planning? I didn't think so. But I was convinced he did know who dreamed this one up, and I was determined to find out who that was if I had to nail Turner to his own barn door.

I had decided to wait in the saloon until evening when there would be fewer people around and less chance of someone interfering in the friendly little discussion I planned on having with Mr. Turner.

"Well, there's no time like the present," I said to the little burro.

The Pawnee was still standing in front of the saloon, his face painted with stripes of ocher and vermillion. He glanced up at me, puzzled-looking, and shrugged.

Adjusting my crutch and bending over, in character, I limped through the town and over to the livery, Cracker in tow. Once inside the stable, I yelled: "Anyone home?" I also rang the bell at the entrance several times for effect.

"Lay off the damn' bell would ya! I'm coming!"

I recognized Turner's voice at once.

"No sense in gettin' all riled up, sonny boy," I said as he approached. "I'm just lookin' fer some lodgings for my old girl, here," I said, gesturing toward Crackers with my head.

"Put her anywhere ya like. Just lay off that bell. I've got a headache."

Hangover is more like it, I thought. Pulling Crackers's pack off, I put her up in the first open stall I found.

"Friend of mine suggested I board ol' Crackers here," I commented while closing the box door.

"Yeah? Who's that?" he asked as if it really was of little importance to him.

"Tall gent with a mean disposition and a big palomino stallion," I answered.

Turner stiffened and looked back at me in surprise. Before he could ask any more questions, I leaned my crutch against the stall and straightened up. Then I hit him square in the jaw so hard he went over backwards like he'd been pole-axed. I had to hand it to him, Turner could take a punch. Most men would have been out for the count, but he managed to roll right over. Holding his jaw in his right hand, he came up onto one knee.

"Where's my palomino, you son-of-a-bitch?" I asked in my own voice, looking around, my fists still clenched.

"It's you. Ah thought you were dead or long gone," he muttered.

"Surprise!" I replied. "Now then, before we continue, I believe I asked you a question." I peeled off my overcoat without taking my eyes off his right hand, which was still holding his jaw. I stupidly failed to notice his left, however, as he grabbed up a fistful of dirt. Next thing knew, he'd flung it at me and bolted for the rear of the barn. I managed to reach him just as he was halfway out the window. I hauled him back inside by his belt and rolled him backwards until he banged up against one of the open stall doors.

"Who are you working for? Why did they frame me?" I asked angrily. "Talk while you still have teeth to chew with."

Turner decided to do his talking with a bucket that was lying nearby, flinging it at me as I stepped back. I deflected it with my forearm and lunged at him. The two of us rolled around for a while, punching, gouging, and kicking. During one of the go-rounds, he somehow managed to end up on top and started choking me. I brought my hands around the outside of his, and, by grabbing his elbows and arching my back, I flung him back over my head. He rolled twice, spun around, got up, and rushed me. I was still on my back, so I brought my knees up and he practically ran right into my feet. I pushed as hard as I could, and Turner was lifted off his feet and thrown backward. He landed hard and had the breath knocked out of him.

I hurried to the front door, looked around, and, after making sure the street was empty, quickly closed the door. I went back to where Turner was and pulled a pitchfork off the wall next to him. I pointed the prongs at his neck and pushed down, just hard enough to make him feel the pain and see the error of his ways.

"Talk, and it better be good," I threatened. "I already know most of it," I lied.

"Anything don't sound right and this fork goes in." I could read the terror in his eyes.

"All right, all right," he squealed. "Ah'm sorry ah done it."

"Go on," I said impatiently.

"This fellow, I think his name's Carl something or other, comes in and gives me fifty dollars to say you rode out of here with loaded saddle-bags. Ah knowd it worn't true, 'cause Ah saw him takin' your horse out o' here that night, but hell, it were fifty dollars."

"You'd lie to frame a man and see him hang for a lousy fifty bucks?" I asked angrily.

"Don't do it please," he cried, apparently assuming I was going to stab him with the pitchfork. "There's more."

"Go on, but make it fast," I replied angrily.

"He pulled a gun and told me if Ah didn't do like he said he'd shoot me in both my kneecaps. Said he'd leave me a cripple from then on. Ah had to do it don't ya see."

I was sure he was too frightened to be lying but pushed a little on his throat again with the fork. "Where's this Carl fellow now? He the one who's got my horse?" I asked angrily as I eased back off the pitchfork.

Turner carefully shook his head. "Only seen him once or twice afore. Works one of the outlying ranches Ah think. Comes into town now and then but pretty much keeps to himself. Don't know him or where he stays. Honest mister, Ah swear all Ah knows is that he was the one who led yore horse out of here that night. Ah don't know nothin' else. Please don't kill me."

I leaned over close to him. "I'll have people watching both you and this livery from now on," I lied again. "You so much as talk to anyone or even sneeze funny and you'll wish all that was done to you was to remove a kneecap or two. Understand?"

Realizing that he might still get out of this alive Dirty Mike began nodding his head violently. "Ah swear to the almighty Ah'll do as you say."

CHAPTER SEVENTEEN

I finished double-checking the barn and I was about to leave when I remembered to fix my disguise. I quietly re-latched the door and backed up. I turned and told Turner to stay put while I went looking in his living quarters, where I hoped to find a mirror or at very least something reflective to help me straighten up.

I succeeded in finding a small mirror on the back wall hanging over a wolf-skin covered cot in the far corner of the room. I needed the make-up kit that I had left in the hotel room to repair the damage done to my disguise during my scuffle with Turner. Fortunately the only harm done was minor and mostly limited to the greasepaint.

I began to wonder how I could get back across town to my room at the inn without attracting too much attention when I noticed a small rag hanging on a nail. I began to feel a cold coming on. Like Al had said, it's all about getting into character and distracting folks' attention away from things you don't want them to see. Kind of like a magician using a pretty girl on stage to keep people's eyes off of his trick moves.

I hoped that as a nondescript old codger I wouldn't stand out too much to begin with, but I figured if someone did get too close, I'd just cover my face up with the rag and pretend to be ill, sneezing and snorting so much that they would turn away.

Crackers was munching contentedly on a pile of hay I'd thrown in her stall. She'd be just fine. With my slouch hat pulled down and the rag over my face, I hoped I would be, too. I had to make it back to my room. If anyone came near me, I was determined to make them think I was more contagious than Typhoid Mary. It was either that or risk swinging from the nearest tree, a fate I fervently wished to avoid.

At one point I literally bumped into the Reverend Fitzpatrick and managed to cough out an "excuse me." I was sure that he must have recognized me but he just walked on without any indication that he had noticed anything amiss.

Luckily for me, the rest of the walk back to the hotel was quiet and uneventful. For some reason, there weren't many people out in the street, and those that were seemed to be going about their own business. I had my hat pulled low, my overcoat back on, and my face covered with the rag. I was reasonably certain that, from a distance, there was nothing about me to attract any attention. Up close, however, the strips of wrinkled rubber pulling away from my face might raise some interest, especially considering those omnipresent Wanted posters of me hanging all over town.

Once or twice, when someone came too close to me, I turned suddenly to look in a window or doubled over to check my boot. I finally made it to the inn and glanced through a side window before entering the lobby. I waited till the coast looked clear and the lobby empty before quickly hurrying on through to the stairs. I was about halfway up the stairwell when I heard Millie's voice, humming, as she came out of the dining room and approached the front desk. With the rag over my face, I glanced quickly over my shoulder. Thankfully she was looking down at the registration ledger and didn't seem to notice me.

As I looked back over my shoulder, I suddenly remembered the other time I'd climbed those stairs, and noticed her talking to that cowboy with the concho-studded belt. It's funny how the mind works, sometimes, but I swear I could suddenly visualize that fellow like he was still standing right there talking to Millie. This time my mind's eye drifted down to his boots. To my surprise, the rowels on his spurs matched the silver on his belt.

I hurried up the stairs to my room. I needed a safe place to stop and think. That very same morning I had considered the possibility of confiding in Millie. I'd hoped to find another ally, but now I wasn't so sure. She seemed so sweet and innocent that it didn't seem possible she would be tied up in all this, but there was no doubt in my mind that the man I saw her flirting with was the very same one who had been preparing to put me in an early grave. There was no doubt that the inn was well run, but it wouldn't be the first enterprise to use stolen funds to pay bills or as a place in which to hide the loot. I scratched my head. It made sense, but somehow just didn't seem right.

I locked the door, took off my overcoat, and unslung my holster from around my shoulder. I then removed my shirt and flopped down on the bed. I was weary of all this and needed to rest. There have been plenty of times in my life when I have been dog tired, but this time my exhaustion was more mental than physical. I was asleep within minutes.

When I awoke the next morning, one of the first things I did was reach for my Colt. I disassembled it, cleaned, and reloaded it. I've found that sometimes it's the simple things that help take your mind off your troubles. Cleaning that pistol helped occupy my time. I don't have a gun fetish like some shootists, it's just that this pistol was truly a work of art and I always found it relaxing to clean and polish it. Plus, it was a special reminder of my grandpa. As corny as it might sound, he was always my hero, as well as my father's father. It was Gramps who gave me this pistol in the first place.

According to my ma, the Mitchell side of our family had been Scottish gunsmiths almost for as long as there had been flint in Scotland. Grandpa Amos Mitchell had worked his way up from being his father's apprentice to joining the army and becoming the youngest master armorer in the history of the Royal Highlanders. Eventually, as is often the case with the young and ambitious, he got a hankering to explore new worlds. Gramps started by shipping out for the colonies, and, when he finished his tour of duty, there he stayed. He eventually started west, turning his back on heather and home. He got as far as Kentucky before he met my grandmother, who at the time was working in a local eatery as a waitress. Grandma was sixteen at the time and, as Gramps used to a tell it, was not only the prettiest thing around, but was also the girl most desperately in need of a Scotsman's hug he ever saw. They were married less than one month after first meeting.

Eventually Gramps established his own shop, figuring that wherever there were guns there would be a need for a good gunsmith. He made a fair living, a great reputation, and over the years lived very happily. Grandma bore him two boys and one girl, my ma.

I do know that Gramps and my pa grew to respect each other, but I don't believe Gramps ever truly forgave Pa for taking away his only daughter. Even I'd have to admit that Ma had inherited her mother's good looks, so it was easy to see why Pa was willing to risk angering the Mitchell clan by whisking their only daughter away. At the time, Pa was just a wandering adventurer. He met Ma while in Gramps's shop, getting his rifle restocked. I guess the Mitchell weaponry and workmanship wasn't the only thing he admired.

Years later, after Grandma died of the plague, Gramps came west to live with us in Colorado. When I turned sixteen, he presented me with a wooden box with the family crest on it. Inside was one of the prettiest pistols I'd ever seen. Gramps had taken a basic stock Navy Colt, a fine revolver in its own right, and made it into a work of art. He started by building up the front sight, filing the sear, smoothing the action, and engraving both the barrel and cylinder. He must have worked on it for months without my knowledge. Sadly it was to be the last birthday we would spend together. Gramps died of a heart attack only six months later.

That was the gun I now held in my hand. I turned it over several times before I reloaded it, remembering a special shooting lesson long ago. "Your grandfather was a true artist, no doubting that," Pa had remarked, "but I'm not all that sure this was such a good idea. A fancy-lookin' pistol like this is just like askin' for trouble. It can get anyone in trouble. Especially a hooligan like you," he teased me. "I best teach you how to use it. Remember, a handgun is a serious tool, it ain't for showin' off. Every man in this country's got a right to protect himself and his family and don't nobody got the right to take it away from you. Not even the government. Our Constitution guarantees that." I recall him pausing a bit for a moment of thought before he continued. "Son, there ain't no good or bad in this thing," he then said, turning the pistol over in his hand. "It's just a tool. Metal's got no morals to it. Only the person holding it does. They say that while God made us all, Colonel Colt made us all equal. Use it wisely and don't ever let me catch you playin' with it. Practice yes . . . play no. You pull it, you use it, you point it, you destroy what it's aiming at. But don't ever shame our family name with it. You hear me, Will?"

"I do, Pa, and you needn't worry," I told him. "I won't never let you down."

"You remember that sword your uncle brought back from the Mexican War?" Pa asked.

"The one with the Spanish writing on the blade?" I had replied, puzzled.

"Right. You know how he got it?"

I nodded, having heard the story before.

When General Zachary Taylor had moved his army into Northern Mexico, the Army of the West that was led by General Stephen W. Kearny marched on Santa Fé, New Mexico. They took the town on August 18, 1846 without a shot being fired. Then, in September, Kearny marched for California and ordered Colonel Doniphan to attack and occupy Chihuahua.

In December of 1846, Colonel Alexander Doniphan led the 1st Regiment of his Missouri Mounted Volunteer Cavalry south from New Mexico to reinforce Wool's division in Northern Mexico. In the longest march in United States military history, this rag-tag group of hard-bitten volunteers eventually fought its way across Mexico. For almost six months they trekked some two thousand miles, all the way down to the Gulf Coast.

"No uniforms, no pay, and no discipline," Uncle Jake had always bragged. "Real rough and tumble they were, but there were no finer fightin' men on this here earth."

Colonel Doniphan was rudely considered an amateur by the regulars. He'd been a lawyer before the war and sort of made up his tactics as he went along, but he was a natural born leader and his men would have followed him to hell, if need be. Uncle Jake was his sergeant major and half of the time Doniphan preferred his counsel to that of his other officers.

At one point, the volunteers marched ninety miles through the hottest stretch of hell on God's earth, the *Jornada del Muerto*, or Journey of the

Dead. They fought at El Brazito and continued south until that fateful day at the Battle of Sacramento. The Missouri Mounted had been following the directions of some local guides, whose loyalties were suspect. Next thing Uncle Jake knew, they were surprised and almost surrounded by three to four times as many Mexicans as there were Missouri troopers.

"There's got to be three to four thousand of 'em, Colonel!" one of Doniphan's lieutenants had cried in panic. "Want us to sound the retreat?"

"We don't take a step back, not one step. Not while I'm still breathing, we don't!" Doniphan had responded angrily.

Then: "Grayson, get your ass over here!" he yelled.

"Yes, sir!" my uncle yelled back, approaching on the run.

"Remember that three line volley fire drill we practiced?"

"Yes, sir," Uncle Jake again replied, snapping to attention.

"Now would be a good time to dismount and put it to use."

"Yes, sir!" he had replied a third time.

"I expect you have about two minutes, so you better make good use of them."

My uncle just stood there awaiting any further orders.

"Now, Sergeant Grayson," the colonel added. "Move!"

When the enemy finally attacked, Colonel Doniphan stood right in the front row, rallying the men, and alongside him was my uncle. When the smoke cleared and the battle was over, the troopers counted over three hundred enemy dead, practically at their feet. There were at least twenty Mexican soldiers in front of my uncle, at least two dead by his own bayonet. After all that carnage, the Missouri Mounted Cavalry had lost only three men. When they later took Chihuahua on March 2, 1847 it was without further incident.

My uncle always said that Colonel Doniphan had saved their hides single-handedly that day, but, regardless of what he claimed, the colonel awarded the victory saber to my uncle, Sergeant Major Grayson. It previously had belonged to the Mexican general-in-charge, and had elegant scrolling on the blade.

"Know what all them fancy words on that sword mean?" Pa had asked me.

"No, sir, I don't."

"Jake told me once. It means . . . 'Don't draw me without reason. Don't sheath me without honor.' Same thing applies with this here pistol. You understand me, son?"

"Yes, Pa," I had answered, feeling humble.

"This Colt will be one of the most important

objects you'll ever own. You do as I say, and I'll stay as proud of you as I am right now."

I have never forgotten his words.

As I lay back on the bed, I wondered how proud Pa would be of what I would have to do to clear my name. I expected there'd be more killing before this thing was resolved.

I got up, re-holstered the pistol, and slung it over my shoulder. I put my shirt back on, sighed, and reluctantly headed over to the mirror. As I've already said, I was getting awfully fed up with this make-up nonsense, but it stood to reason that if Millie knew who was wearing those fancy roweled spurs, then she might know where to find him. I needed to talk to her, only now there was no way I would reveal who I really was until I had all the facts.

CHAPTER EIGHTEEN

"Missy, I need to find someone, and I thought you might be able to help me," I said, approaching Millie down in the lobby. Once again, I was speaking with my hoarse old-timer's voice. I kept my hat on and my head lowered when I addressed her, behind the reception desk.

"Well, of course I'll help you, Mister Walters," she replied. "Or at least I'll try. We get a lot of people coming through here, but please realize that not everyone signs our ledger. Some only come in here for a meal in our restaurant. Who is it you are trying to find?"

I fiddled with my mouth like I was adjusting a set of false teeth. "Don't rightly know his name. Some fellow I met a while back while out on the trail. He had a real nice rifle that I took a fancy to, and he said he would sell it to me if I ever had enough cash. He's the fellow who told me about how nice this inn was," I explained.

"Why, thank you," she replied sweetly.

I found it hard to understand how this pretty young thing could be tied up with bank robbers.

"Not at all. 'Tis the truth. Said he was a real close friend o' your'n."

"Really? And you met him out on the trail?"

she asked, a puzzled look on her face. "Who was he? What does he look like?"

"Oh, you can't miss him. Real young whipper-snapper. Tall sort, dark, with a small moustache. Sported a fancy belt full of them round silver things the Mexes favor. Had them big silver rowels on his spurs, too. They're a bit harsh on horses for my taste, though, iffen you ask me."

Her face darkened and her attitude changed. "Oh, him."

"Something wrong, missy?" I asked.

"It's nothing, Mister Walters," she replied. "It's just that I believe I know the man you're referring to, and I find him to be rather disagreeable."

"Really? He sort of implied you two was quite an item," I said.

She became rather agitated. "I'm sure he did, but, I assure you, nothing could be further from the truth. His name is Raul. His last name is Hunte, but I believe he is half Mexican." She shook her head in disgust. "He comes into town from time to time, and, when he does, he always tries to force his attention on me. You know the type. Always leans over my counter, trying to get closer to a lady than is appropriate." She actually shuddered. "I'm sorry to speak ill of your friend . . . it's just that he scares me some-times."

I was relieved. Maybe I could still trust my instincts about people, after all.

"Ain't no friend o' mine," I stated, with a shrug. "Like I said, I just want to buy that rifle of his."

"There's a store in town that sells several kinds of rifles. I could gladly direct you there. It would certainly save you a trip," she offered helpfully.

I wondered why womenfolk always have to complicate even the simplest of things. "No, missy, but thank you anyway. An ol' codger like me knows a bargain when he sees one, and I got me a hankering for that particular rifle, iffen he still wants to sell it, that is," I replied. "Any idea where I might find this Raul fellow? He here in town?"

"Don't believe so. I would surely have seen him by now, if he were," she answered, shaking her head and turning her lips up. "He bought the Jefferson place about two months ago. I expect that's where you will probably find him."

"The Jefferson place? Sorry, that don't ring no bell. See, I ain't from around here," I reminded her.

"Oh, I'm sorry, I forgot for a moment. They were such nice folks. Everyone liked the Jeffersons, but they just up and moved away rather suddenly one day. If I remember correctly, it was shortly thereafter that Raul came in saying he had bought their ranch. It was quite a surprise to many of us. Missus Jefferson used to make the finest pies, and we often sold them in our restaurant."

"That so?" I replied, a little frustrated with her long explanations. "So, is this place far?"

She giggled. "Sorry, I was rambling wasn't I? Let's see . . . the ranch is about four miles outside of town. Head up the trail to the north and go straight till you come to the first fork in the road. Take the right branch and it will take you directly to his ranch."

"Much obliged." I raised my hand to my hat as if to say thanks, turned, and hobbled out the door.

Once outside, I stopped short in my tracks. It suddenly occurred to me that I didn't have a horse, and, although my ankle was better now, I didn't feel much like walking the four miles. Delilah was back with Al, and it would probably be faster to walk, than to ride Crackers. There wasn't any stage due today, and it probably didn't go by the ranch, anyway. I needed transportation and I wanted it fast, but the question was where to find a spare horse.

Horses . . . you find them at a livery stable. Once I made that connection, the rest was simple. I'd just borrow Turner's horse. After all, he sure as hell wasn't going to argue with me.

I found Mike Turner hiding in his office and had him point out his horse. It was a chestnut gelding standing in the last stall at the back of the livery. I couldn't help but notice that his horse had the cleanest stall in the barn. I needed his horse regardless, but I'd probably bring it back eventually. Either that or I'd be hanged as a horse thief. Right after they hanged me for robbing the bank, that is.

The chestnut wasn't bad tempered, quite the opposite, but he had an old bowed tendon on his right foreleg and some healed shin splints. He was cow hocked to boot. I figured he'd get me where I wanted to go all right, but we wouldn't break any world records getting there. Right then and there I sorely missed my palomino stallion. He was fast as greased lightning and had no back up or quit in him.

I saddled the chestnut and led him out of the barn, and then mounted up. From what Millie had said, I reckoned I could make it to the ranch where this fellow Raul was supposed to be in a couple of hours. I might have made it in less time on my palomino, but not on this horse. I looked around, and once I'd made sure the coast was clear, I galloped out of town.

Millie's directions weren't hard to follow, and I soon found the cut-off she had referred to. The ranch was about a half hour farther up the pike. I pulled up short of the ranch and rode the chestnut in a semi-circle around the property, looking for any signs of activity. I tried not to ride out in the open, preferring to use the trees as cover so as not to be as visible from the cabin. I counted only one horse tied out in front of the cabin and noticed that there was smoke rising from the chimney.

There was nothing out of the ordinary about the ranch as far as I could see. It had a perimeter fence around it that appeared to be well made, and there was a large set of horns over the entranceway to the ranch. I could ride around the place trying to find a way to sneak in, but with only one horse out front and a closed-up cabin, I didn't think I needed to waste that much time. Raul probably wouldn't hear me coming. If I rode up quickly and quietly, I might be able to brace him, head-on. Of course, I also knew what could happen if I just charged in and kicked down the door. There was a good chance of getting shot, especially since I didn't know what kind of reflexes Raul had. I was about to check my pistol when I remembered my holster was around my shoulder, not my waist. I was still in costume and going in as a feeble old man might give me the advantage I needed. I might still get shot, but then if you've got to die, it's better to die old than young. I broke out in a grin at the thought.

I put a heel to the chestnut and headed right toward the cabin at a slow jog. I hitched the horse next to the chocolate roan that was tied up, and then knocked on the door. It opened, and, after giving me the once over, Raul finally came out onto the stoop.

"What do you want, old man?" he asked, blocking the doorway.

"Don't rightly know iffen I got the right place," I answered, "but there's this pretty young thing back in town, name of Millie, what sent me out here to deliver a message to some feller named Raul. That you?"

He looked surprised. "That so?" he said, then he nodded and broke out in a wicked grin. "Millie, huh? What did she say?"

I didn't answer him right off. I wanted a look inside the cabin before I braced him. I didn't want some other gang member, hiding behind the door, to get the drop on me.

"Sonny, you gonna make me stand out here or you gonna let me rest my old bones on one of them chairs inside. That long ride didn't do me no good, you know. Fellow comes all this way just to deliver some silly girl's message to a beau and you don't even offer him a jug. Folks just ain't hospitable like they used to be," I said, shaking my head while rambling on.

He shrugged. "Sure, old-timer, come on in."

As I walked past him, I began to unbutton my greatcoat.

"Hey, wait a moment," he said suddenly. "What are you doing with Mike's horse?" The thought hadn't occurred to me before his

227

comment, but there was always a possibility that someone familiar with the town might recognize the horse as belonging to Turner. I had to act fast, so, as I brushed past him, I grabbed his shirt near the scruff of his neck and yanked him into the cabin, spinning him backwards. Raul went sprawling against the far wall, and by the time he turned to face me, my pistol was in his face.

"Who the hell are you, and what do you want?" he growled.

"Some answers about the rest of your murdering, bank-robbing gang. And I better get them, or you'll quickly learn the meaning of pain." I pulled off my overcoat and tore the wig from my head.

"It's you!" he exclaimed, recognizing me at once. "So, you're not dead after all!"

If I needed anything more to convince me of his guilt, that comment clinched it. Back in town, at the hotel, when I looked down the steps, Raul had been too busy sparking Millie to notice me. He might have recognized me from one of those Wanted posters, but all the ones I'd seen had said I was alive and on the run. Only those bushwhackers, who had attacked me that night, would think me dead from the fall.

"Guess Lazarus ain't the only one coming back. Surprised, huh?"

I was standing near the door, facing into the cabin, with my pistol leveled at Raul when the lights went out. Not the ones in the cabin, the ones in my head.

CHAPTER NINETEEN

When I came to, not long after, I found myself sprawled on the floor. I immediately noticed two things. One was that my hands were tied behind my back, and the other was that my head hurt. It hurt a lot. I hadn't opened my eyes yet, but my ears were working just fine and what I heard had me plenty worried. Raul was talking to someone about disposing of the body. This time I didn't have to think very hard on whose body they were once again referring to.

"Do it right this time, would you?" someone said.

I opened my eyelids a crack and caught a glimpse of the same cowboy with the red hatband I'd seen that night back in town. He must have been in the barn when I rode up to the ranch. Millie hadn't mentioned anyone else living at the ranch, and, since I'd only seen the one horse out front, I assumed that Raul was alone. Wrong assumption. Like my uncle Jake used to tell me, writing it out on a piece of paper this way: *Assume means making an Ass out of U and Me.*

I tried to free my hands without making any noise, but they were too tightly bound. Something about this situation seemed awfully familiar, and I didn't like it one bit. Then again, what worked once might work again, so I played opossum like before, hoping for some remote chance to survive.

"I'll go back to town and fill the boss in on all this, and then I'll make sure this big galoot didn't leave anyone back there to check up on him. Once the party is over and the boss leaves town, I'll come back, so we can start clearing out of here."

It was the one with the red hatband doing the talking.

"What about the loot?" Raul asked.

"He's carrying it with him, like always," was the reply. "Safely packed away in the buckboard. We split it up when we all get back together, and not until. Everyone's got to be there or nobody gets any . . . that's the deal. Meanwhile, you make sure this one's dead and buried for good this time. No screw ups, you got me?"

"I got it, Carl," Raul replied grimly, "but remember, don't interrupt the boss till after the ceremony is over. We don't want anything to bugger his excuse for leaving town. Better get going. I got this covered."

I heard the door slam shut and the sound of a revolver cylinder spinning. I wanted to think over what had just been said, but first I had to buy some time. I had to think fast or forget all those plans I had for fame, fortune, and fun with Millie.

Millie . . . As much as Raul was smitten with her, mentioning Millie just might buy me some time. I rolled over and shook my head. Raul was looking down at me with a sadistic grin on his face and a Remington six-shooter in his hand. I had to distract him and get him talking.

"Well, it's a damn' shame," I said to him.

"What is?" he asked.

"I'm just thinking that it's a shame to go out like this . . . hands tied, shot by a low-life coward who's too afraid to fight me fair."

"Nice try," he said, smiling, "but my mama didn't raise no fools. You got any prayers, now's the time to say them." He started to point the pistol in my direction.

"I guess Millie was right, then," I added quickly. I could see him raise an eyebrow.

"Millie? What's she got to do with this?"

I had been right. His curiosity had kicked in.

"How do you suppose I knew where to find you?" I replied. "She and I have been seeing each other for a while now," I boasted.

"All the more reason to shoot you," he sneered.

"You're proving my point," I answered. "Millie said she always suspected you might be the type to shoot an unarmed man. Tell you what, I'll make you a deal. If you won't untie me, then how about fighting me like this?"

He laughed. "What . . . with your hands tied?"

"Fair enough deal," I replied, nodding. "Look

232

at it this way, I sort of get a chance . . . not much of one I'll admit . . . but at the very least I get to go out on my feet like a man, instead of on my knees. You on the other hand still get to kill me, only now you also get to beat the crap out of the man who stole your girl. That is unless you're afraid that you can't fight a man with his hands tied behind his back." I laughed back at him.

"That'll be the day. I can beat you from now to Sunday with or without them ropes," he replied angrily.

"Then put the gun down and get on with it, big mouth," I goaded.

He reholstered the pistol, took off his belt, and set it across the back of a nearby chair.

"I'm gonna enjoy this," he said, clenching his fists.

"I'm sure you will," I said, standing up with some difficulty. "By the way, ever heard of *savate*?"

"Who's he?" Raul asked as he moved in.

I brought my right leg up in an arc, swinging my hip from the outside to my inside and catching his head with the side of my boot. Raul's head snapped sideways and he went flying to my left.

"Not who, Raul, what. It's a form of French kickboxing."

He got back to his feet and swung at my head. I leaned backward as far as the ropes around my wrists would allow and push-kicked straight forward hitting him square in the chest. His fist barely missed my face, but my kick managed to lift him up and fling him backward off his feet.

During the months I'd spent with my miner friends in Bannock, we often passed the nights and rainy days playing cards. But one can only play so much, so we often looked for other ways to pass the time. Jock O'Reilly had spent a great part of his life in New Orleans and up along the Mississippi River and was a *savate* expert.

Savate originally started as a form of street fighting in Marseille and Paris and was sometimes called *causson* or slipper, after them funny shoes the French sailors wear. Jock O'Reilly originally learned it from the many Frenchmen who frequented the bars and casinos where he lived. Even as old as he was, he could clean my clock without working up a sweat. Naturally I had to convince him to teach me. Once he gave in, we practiced about two hours every day, and, since then, I'd gotten pretty good at it myself.

I thought Raul was still catching his breath when he suddenly lunged at me. I reacted by turning, and gave him a side kick, which caught the side of his ribcage. I continued spinning and hook-kicked the side of his head with the back of my heel. He was still standing when I knocked his feet out from under him with a leg sweep. As he was falling, I caught his chin with my knee in the leg version of an uppercut. I could hear his neck snap as he dropped dead in a pile in front of me.

I looked down at his body unemotionally. Remorse was not one of my major emotions at the moment. Raul had let his anger get the better of him, and, as a result, had given me a chance. Lucky for me he forgot the old saying that no good deed goes unpunished. I saw my Bowie knife on the table and retrieved it before sitting down in one of the chairs. It took me awhile to cut the ropes away since it was awkward trying to hold on to the knife behind my back and cut at the same time. But I managed it in time.

Once free, I sheathed the knife and reholstered my pistol. I headed for the door loaded for bear and angry as one to boot. While I cut the ropes I had time to think about what had been said between Raul and Carl and now knew who was behind all this. There was only one person who could be the gang's ringleader. While I was tied up, Carl had said their boss was at a party, but was planning on leaving town right afterward. Raul then cautioned him not to interrupt the boss at the ceremony. There was only one person they could have meant. The same person who had convinced the whole town that I had robbed the bank, and had then made a clean getaway. Only one person could have pulled all this off. Sheriff Jeremy Kent.

It stood to reason that he must be marrying the

widow Elliott as an excuse to leave town. I felt sorry for her. She seemed so nice and behaved so elegantly, and now, because of me, she was likely to wind up a widow for the second time, even before beginning her honeymoon.

I looked at the Regulator clock on the cabin wall. Maybe if I hurried, I could get back before they got hitched and spare her some grief.

I was mad and my sore ankle hurt like hell. In my anger, I kicked open the cabin door, tore off the remnants of my costume, and wiped off my make-up as best I could. I'd had enough of that for good. I re-buckled the holster, this time on my waist, and double-checked my Navy Colt. It felt good to wear it on my hip again, where it belonged, instead of slung around my shoulder. I took a deep breath and resolved to end this affair once and for all, even if it meant killing anyone who got in my way.

Although I needed to get back to town in a hurry, I debated for a moment whether to ride the same slow chestnut I'd come in on, or to switch to the roan that was still tied up in front of the cabin. I knew what the chestnut was capable of, but that roan had better conformation and looked to be a better choice for a hard and fast ride. It was then I heard a familiar nicker coming from the barn out back.

The relationship between a working rider and his horse is something unique and hard to describe. It doesn't matter if it is a cowpoke and his pony or a city milkman and the cold blood that pulls his cart. There is a special dependence on one another that develops over time. I've seen thirsty men give their mounts the last sip from the canteen and known crooks to surrender rather than risk having their horse shot.

I remembered the time I was riding down a steep slope coming out of some woods back home. I had been forced to change course three times before that, because, every time I came out of that one patch of forest, I ran smack into a gorge of sorts—kind of like a deep canal that was too wide to jump and too steep to walk down into. It seemed to snake around in a big circle. Either the woods were too thick to get through, or I kept hitting that gorge. For a while, I was afraid I'd be trapped. I couldn't just backtrack, because I had gotten into this situation by taking what I thought was a short cut that entered this particular section of woods by a funnel-like path that was wide going in but came out through the trees into the open by a very narrow margin. I couldn't even find it again if I tried.

After the fourth attempt to get free of this maze, I finally came out on a clear path that lead downhill to an open field. It looked fine, and I urged the horse down. For some unexplained reason, he wasn't having any of it. "What's this about, fellow?" I had wondered. "Come on I can smell bacon frying on the pan. Let's go, I want to get back," I had urged him, nudging him gently with my right spur and leaning forward. "Get up," I kept repeating. Again, he played mule on me and refused to budge. I cocked an eye once again at that slope and it looked fine to me, not too steep, no chuckholes or slick spots. I should have trusted the horse, but my stomach was growling and I was impatient. There's a reason folks speak of horse sense.

"All right, be that way," I had said out loud as I tightened up. I took hold of my rein and flicked his side with it at the same time I gave him both spurs. That stallion bolted down the slope and then sprang into the longest jump he'd ever made, and we both flew out over what I thought was a wide open field. Trouble was, it wasn't clear, nor dry for that matter. A previous wind storm had blown a layer of dust and debris over the water. By the time I had arrived the wind was so calm and the top layer so thick that it made it appear to be solid ground. My horse knew better.

When we landed it was with a frightening splash, and the next thing I knew the horse was up to his ears. The combination of canal water and dirt made a thick muck that had the consistency of glue. It was an unreal experience. There I was sitting on a horse, totally buried in mud, and not budging. I couldn't tell if his legs were broken or if he was just stuck. Somehow or another, I slid off the saddle and tried to remove his cinch. All that mud made it impossible to get under the saddle to undo the knot. Since his reins were too short to reach the other side of the canal, I removed my lasso and tossed a loop over his head and neck in the form of a makeshift halter. I made my way to the other side with great effort. It was too thick to swim and too wet to walk, and it was a struggle just to take a step.

Once on dry ground, I pondered the next move. My palomino stallion had only his head showing above water. The rest of the horse, along with saddle and gear, was totally buried in mud. I had no idea what was going on with his hoofs, but I had no choice. I said a small prayer and, pulling on the rope, gave a loud whistle.

I don't know how he managed it, but he came up out of that ooze and leaped clear to the other side of the canal. In fact, he went right over me and I had to fall onto my back to avoid getting hit by his hoofs. In doing so, I dropped the rope and half expected him to hit the ground running in panic. I had every right to expect a long walk alone. Instead, he came to a stop, shook himself off, and walked back to me.

As I checked him over, he nuzzled me playfully. Except for the loss of one shoe and my dignity, thankfully, we were unharmed. It took me two days to clean the mud out of my saddle, pack, and boots, a penance I was more than willing to perform for the sin of thinking I knew more about the trail than my horse had.

Some might call it love, but I don't think that really explains it. I've loved family members and can even say I truly loved the dog I grew up with. But with horses, it isn't the same sort of feeling. It's not quite as automatic, as say, with a puppy. With a working horse there is a different sort of bond, it's a mutual respect and a need that continually grows. A good cayuse sort of fills an empty spot in some of us and becomes part of you.

Just like I'd recognize a long lost family member's voice, I immediately recognized that stallion's nicker. I turned and ran to the barn as best I could and flung open the door. There in the middle stall was my palomino. I was never so happy as when I opened his stall, and he immediately began to nudge me with his head. I led him out of the stall and checked him over. He appeared well grained and cared for. Thankfully Mike Turner and his low appreciation for animal husbandry wasn't typical of the members of this gang.

I looked around until I finally found my tack in the far corner of the barn, and then quickly saddled up. My Henry rifle was still in its scabbard. I levered a round out, and then replaced it to check the action. It was loaded and working fine.

Once outside the barn, I can't describe how good it felt to be well heeled and in my own saddle, astride my own mount. Even after all I'd been through, I felt like I could wrestle a bear with an arm tied behind me and eat him afterwards. I put a spur to the stallion, and we shot off toward town.

As we started off, I felt sort of like a fellow in that dime Beadle magazine of Al's. I had a date with destiny. *Well, maybe so,* I thought, grinning, *but, if I had anything to say in the matter, Sheriff Kent is going to have a date with the devil.*

CHAPTER TWENTY

The ride into town gave me some time to plan my stand. It stood to reason that the sheriff would be surrounded by half the town. If I went in shooting, I'd be dead before I could even begin to explain what I knew. Most of the men in town went around armed. Who could blame them. For one thing, you can't survive out here without knowing how to hunt, and most of the men in town were probably ex-soldiers from the war, to boot. They'd know how to handle a gun and would hit what they aimed at, and they'd be aiming at me.

An honest man wouldn't have it any other way. People have a God-given right to protect themselves and their families the best way they can. Hell, it's so important they even stuck it in the Bill of Rights. I understood that. Once in town it would be practically impossible for me to make my case with a passel of armed citizens, if they thought I was a dangerous criminal.

If I wasn't shot on the spot, Sheriff Kent would make sure I was lynched from the nearest tree. That crowd idolized their sheriff, and, without a chance to explain things, my neck would be stretched longer than John Brown's. Once a lynch mob gets going, it's like a swarm of angry bees. Besides, my time in Blue Lake Ridge had already convinced me that few of the townsfolk were willing even to consider explanations that didn't agree with their preconceived notions.

I needed some way to attract the town's attention. Something that would get them to stop and listen to me before Sheriff Kent had a chance to shut me up. Something to buy me time. Unfortunately I reached town before I could work out exactly what that thing might be.

I undid the tie-down thong from my holster and rode my horse at a slow walk straight toward the saloon. I could see the crowd emptying onto the street and lining up to escort the newly wedded couple to their buckboard. Off to my right, I could see that Pawnee Indian, still standing on the plank walk. I stopped and glanced at him. To my surprise he winked at me. Now I've been around a lot of Indians in my time, and have had them give me just about every gesture in the book, including throwing a tomahawk at my head, but I couldn't recall one ever winking at me. He stood there with that red blanket around his chest without making any threatening moves, so I just nodded back and turned my attention to the crowd.

Down the street, the sheriff and his new bride were coming out of the saloon. Just as I expected, there was a large crowd milling around them, wishing them well. Personally I would have chucked a brick at Kent, if I'd had one. Angrily I pulled my Henry rifle from the scabbard.

Life takes some funny twists and turns sometimes, and this was one of them. My palomino was as steady a horse as you'd expect to find, but he was a stallion. There must have been a mare in heat around or something spooked him, because he chose that precise moment to rear straight up on his back legs. How I managed to stay in the saddle, I can't tell you, but it sure must have been quite a sight. Kind of like that Masked Avenger Al had told me about.

There I was, right out in front of that crowd, free of my disguise, walking my horse down the street on two legs, straight toward them. To say they were stunned would be an understatement. But it was just the break I needed. When my horse finally settled back down, I yelled out: "Martin . . . Martin Turnbull . . . you here?"

A buzz of commentary worked its way through the crowd, and Bull stepped cautiously out.

Behind him I heard the sheriff yell out my name, but so far nobody had moved.

"Catch!" I yelled, and tossed Bull my rifle. "You once said you owed me one, Bull. All I'm asking now is that you to keep the crowd back long enough for them to hear me out."

"Why should I?" he asked.

I don't know if he was acting suspicious because he truly was or if he was just acting like it for the benefit of the crowd. But I still had to answer him. "I didn't rob that bank and I believe you know it. Think about it, would a guilty man come back here and then toss you a loaded rifle to shoot him with?" I asked. For a moment we just stared at each other.

He levered a round into the chamber, and, looking right at me, raised the rifle up. I can tell you the hairs on the back of my neck stood straight up, but he suddenly swung around to face the others.

"Don't nobody move!" he yelled. "I want to hear this man out."

"They're probably in on it together!" yelled the sheriff. "Come on, get 'em, men!"

"There's women and children here!" I cried. "I don't want to see anyone who's innocent get hurt."

It was then that the reverend jumped out in front of the crowd with his Bible held high. He stood right alongside Bull and shouted: "Stop, I beseech you! Let's hear him out before any shooting starts!"

"Millie, if you're somewhere in the crowd there, please, get the womenfolk and children back inside!" I shouted.

There was method in my madness. For a brief moment any parent present would turn their attention to their children, rather than rushing at me. Also, it made me appear to be more concerned about the welfare of the families than was their precious sheriff.

"Why would a guilty man return?" I yelled as I dismounted from my horse. "More importantly why would a man coming to town, flush with gold, rob cash from a bank the day after he arrives? If I rode in on this horse without a pack mule, where would I hide the explosives necessary to blow a hole that big in the bank?" I paused letting my words sink in. "And how the hell would a stranger to town know precisely when the fireworks were set to go off so that he could time the explosion of the dynamite?"

"Don't listen to him men!" Kent shouted back. "We know he's guilty. We got witnesses."

The crowd was beginning to part. I noticed the sheriff starting to pick up the reins and I knew right then that he was going to bolt.

"Men, you let that buckboard take off and you may never see your money again," I warned them quickly. "The sheriff was behind this all along and I can prove it. Those witnesses of his were all part of the gang. They were all in on it from the get-go."

Two of Turnbull's friends, the ones I'd seen in the salon, quickly grabbed the reins to the buckboard.

"The money is hidden somewhere in the buckboard . . . probably buried under all those nice presents you gave them," I explained.

I turned my attention to June Elliott, who was the only woman who had remained outside. "Sorry to ruin your honeymoon, Missus Elliott, but your new husband, the noble town sheriff, is actually a bushwhacker and a bank robber. He was just using you as a way to get out of town with the money. Better that you know it now, I guess."

"You're crazy!" Kent yelled as he got down from the buckboard, and then turned to face me. "This is ridiculous. I arrest you in the name of the law. Get his guns, men."

"If any of you know Al Kleiner, he can vouch for me," I replied.

"Then he's in on this it, too," Kent answered. I could see him releasing his pistol thong as he spoke.

"Al Kleiner?" someone yelled. "No way. I know Al, and he ain't got a crooked bone in his body."

"Hey, you all, lookey here what I found!" It was one of Bull's friends, the fat one who was yelling. He was shuffling through the back of the buckboard. "There's some money here . . . plenty. It still had got them paper bands the bank uses to tie up the cash."

The men in the crowd were stunned, and slowly they began to separate, forming a circle around the two of us.

I gestured to the reverend and Turnbull to back away.

"Damn you, Grayson . . . you'll rot in hell!" Kent cried out.

All of a sudden a blast rang out behind me. I turned to find the Pawnee standing over the lifeless body of a cowboy with a red hatband.

In my anger and haste I'd forgotten about Carl, Raul's partner, being in town.

"I spied him hiding up in a balcony," the Pawnee explained, "all set to backshoot you or anyone who got in the sheriff's way."

I looked at the Indian, studying his face for a second, when I noticed he winked at me again. Then it hit me like timber. I knew that voice and the double-barreled side-by-side shotgun he had hidden under his red blanket looked very familiar.

"Got your back, Will!" he yelled.

He may have been a Pawnee Indian on the outside, but it was Al Kleiner's voice coming from the inside.

"Well I'll be damned." I laughed. "I thought we agreed you were going to stay out of all this."

"Pawnee" Al Kleiner shook his head and laughed. "I decided I just couldn't let you do this alone. Besides I didn't want to miss the action."

"Thanks, Al . . . but I can take it from here," I replied gratefully.

Sheriff Jeremy Kent looked at me with fire in his eyes.

"I'll kill you for this," he said angrily. His

voice was cold, but his eyes burned with fire and hate.

"Maybe so, but either way you're going down."

I could feel the tension in the air as time seemed to slow to a standstill. I watched Kent's fingers tighten around his Remington six-shooter, and watched his eyelids twitch. I don't truly remember thumbing back the hammer on my Colt, or even drawing it for that matter, but I do remember seeing his gun smoke and feeling the awful blast as the bullet hit me. The strange thing is that I was sure I had beaten him to the draw. As I went down, I saw his lifeless body sprawled in the street. I was on my knees when another shot rang out.

Through the fog I thought I saw June Elliott walking toward me with one of those little Derringers in her hand. It appeared to be smoking, and all I remember, before I passed out, was how she too started falling, face forward into the dirt.

Looking up through the dust in my eyes, I noticed the reverend standing over me, a smoking revolver in his right hand. After belting the pistol, he extended his hand and helped me, slowly, to my feet. Blood was dripping down my shirt from the wound in my shoulder. My left arm was numb, but I knew that sooner or later the pain would inevitably return.

"Great," I mumbled angrily, holding my left

shoulder with my right hand. "Just as it was finally healing." The reverend led me over to a bench on the walkway in front of the saloon.

"June, is she . . . ?" I asked. The reverend nodded grimly.

"You had a gun all along?" I said. "I just don't get it. What made you finally decide to jump in?" I was both surprised and curious.

He bent over and retrieved the oversize Bible he'd left on the ground next to the sidewalk bench. Opening the book, he reached in and pulled out a small badge and some identification. I noticed that the book had been hollowed out, with what remained of the pages pasted together to form a secret storage compartment inside. That's where he had carried his revolver all along. I looked up at him, nonplussed.

"Real name's Marcus," he said. "James Marcus. Fitzpatrick was just an alias."

I looked at his badge. "You're a private detective?" I exclaimed in disbelief.

"I am," he said. "I'm here on what they call detached duty."

"How's that again?" I winced from the growing pain. "I'm afraid I don't understand." My shoulder was just beginning to act up, but I knew it was going to get a lot worse later.

"You might say this one was personal," he replied, closing the book. "See this isn't the first time this bunch has pulled this gambit. They were a very clever and dangerous group. I've been trailing them going on three years now."

I winced again when I shifted.

"Here, we need to get you some medical attention," he said, helping to support me.

One of the townsfolk ran to fetch the doctor while I removed my shirt, folded it as best I could, and for the time being used it to plug the bullet hole in my shoulder.

Al came over, smiled and pulled the scalp lock off his head along with its rubber bald-headed cover.

Detective Marcus looked shocked at first, but quickly caught on. They both laughed as the two of them helped me to my feet, and then we all started off toward the doc's office.

"Kent was the brains behind the whole scheme," Marcus explained. "They'd pick a town, and then he'd ride in alone in order to establish himself in some sort of position of authority. Might be in a town needing a new sheriff like this one, or maybe he'd hire on as deputy. Once he claimed to be a Wells Fargo officer and another time he was supposedly a bank detective. His real name was Bodine."

"Bodine?" I shook my head. "Name doesn't ring a bell."

"No reason it should. He was the slippery sort . . . the kind who never allows himself to get pinned down on paper. See, once he rode into a town, he always worked his way into becoming a figure of respectability. As soon as he'd set himself up in some sort of respectful job, he'd survey the local bank or express office, usually claiming it was as part of his new assignment, and then he'd send word to the others in his gang. They would then filter in and take up residence throughout the town."

"Sounds pretty elaborate," Al remarked.

Marcus nodded his head. "Got to admit, it was very well thought out. But with all their money collected from previous robberies they could afford to take their own sweet time. If they couldn't find jobs, well, then, by God, they'd make them, like buying out a livery cheap or scaring away a shopkeeper so they could take over his place."

"Or arranging to have a sheriff trampled to death in a cow pen late at night," I remarked, thinking out loud.

"Say, that makes sense," Al replied, stroking his chin and nodding in agreement.

We arrived at the doctor's office and they settled me in. The doctor had just begun to examine my wound when I gestured for him to stop.

"Please, Doc, could you wait just a moment . . . I'd like to hear the rest of this first."

"We ought to get right at that shoulder, son," he argued. "These things can be nasty sometimes."

"I'll survive," I replied while gritting my teeth. "Seems I always do."

"I'll vouch for that," Al remarked.

"I don't like it much," the doctor replied, but, after looking at the three of us, he was forced to admit defeat. "All right, go on, but make it quick, will you?"

"Right, Doc," Marcus said before continuing. "Now let's see, where was I? Oh, yeah, when the gang was finally in position and ready, June Elliott would arrive to help them snooker some innocent victim."

"Like she did with me," I added, feeling irritation now in addition to the pain.

He nodded. "Right, like she did with you. But first, they had to establish a reason for her arrival and an excuse for her continued stay in town. This time her alibi was created by posing as a widow lady passing through town on her way back home who decides to stay for the holiday festivities. Usually she would then coincidentally . . . or should I say conveniently . . . become a witness to the robbery. She can be very convincing, believe me."

In spite of the pain I had to chuckle. "Trust me I do. I know very well from firsthand experience and a big knot on my head just how believable she was," I replied recalling our meeting that night in the street.

Marcus continued with his tale. "So, after

spending some time with the sheriff as part of his official duties, or with whoever Bodine was playing at the time, they would just happen to fall in love. Pretty clever, eh?"

"Sounds like it would make a fancy New York drama," Al said, obviously impressed.

The detective looked quizzically at Al.

"He used to be an actor," I inserted.

"Oh, so that explains it," Marcus said, then chuckled.

"Can we get started now?" the doctor asked impatiently.

"Just another moment, Doc, I need to hear this," I pleaded.

"Well, it's against my better judgment, but go ahead," he answered. But then added: "I'd kinda like to hear the rest of this, too."

The detective pulled up a chair and continued his story. "During the last job they pulled, the story used was that she was on her way to visit her sick aunt. But regardless of the pretext, she'd always make a point of letting just about everyone in town know that because her income was limited, she was forced to stick around for a while before continuing her travels."

"Let me guess," Al piped in. "The whole time that she's sparkin' the lawman, or whoever, she's also complaining about how much she misses being home, or how she'd much rather be back in the East than some small Western cow town."

"Right you are," the detective continued. "See that way, later on it would give the two of them the excuse they needed to pull out. Meanwhile, the gang would single out some stranger who was unlucky enough to be in the wrong place at the wrong time to be their scapegoat. The widow Elliott would then either invite him up to her place late at night or lure the poor soul somewhere where the others could jump him from behind."

"Like they did with me," I remarked in disgust.

"Right again," he confirmed.

"In my case I saw a woman alone at night in need of an escort through a dark alley," I explained. "Noble ol' me just had to rush to the rescue like a real live Sir Lancelot. Once I was in that alley, they whacked me from behind."

"Don't be too hard on yourself, son," Al remarked. "Hard not to be taken in by someone with her looks."

"Al's right. You're lucky," the detective commented. "As far as I can tell, you're the only one who managed to survive this gang."

"Just hard-headed I guess," I joked.

"Once they had ambushed their chosen victim, they would ditch his body, turn his horse loose somewhere far out of town, rob the bank, and then blame the theft on the notorious missing stranger," Marcus continued. "In some towns, June would give testimony to the effect that she had heard a noise late at night and, upon looking out the window, had seen the stranger hightailing it out of town. Her story, coming from a seemingly innocent and impartial observer, would lend credibility to the accusations gang members made against the missing stranger."

"And once they're convinced, angry mobs, especially those who have had their life savings stolen, don't usually stop to logically consider other possibilities," I observed.

"No they don't," he agreed. "Anyway, Bodine, in the role of sheriff, or bank official, or deputy, would rush the posse into a wild-goose chase in search of the phantom bank robber, or should I say their now dead scapegoat. If anyone began to question things he would probably be talked down by the sheriff and the other gang members planted in the posse."

My shoulder was really aching now, so I let the doctor begin cleaning the wound.

"It would always be a fruitless search for the posse," Marcus noted, "but, of course, they didn't know it at the time. Bodine would lead those posses around in circles, all the while appearing anxious to help the townsfolk try to find a robber he knew perfectly well didn't exist. Folks always spoke highly of how much he had dedicated himself to getting their money back. He left no stone unturned. No way a town would ever suspect him of anything."

I shook my head in disbelief at the extent of his deviousness.

"So how did they get out of all those towns afterward?" Al asked.

"Near as I can figure it, June Elliott provided their out," he explained. "See the whole gang couldn't just take off right after the robbery. People might get suspicious if that number of folks all left town at the same time, especially so soon after a hold-up. Bodine was a perfectionist. He wanted things to go flawlessly, no trails left behind. Nope, they were far too clever to just pull right out. Besides, since they weren't strapped for cash, time was their friend."

"I think I'm catching your drift," I said.

Detective Marcus paused a moment to remove a white kerchief from his pocket, and then proceeded to wipe his brow. "That's the slick part. Nobody ever suspected any of them. It was very frustrating. I couldn't get anyone to help. I had no evidence. Anything I had to offer to the authorities was just one man's opinion, and a layman's theories not very appreciated, especially in an angry town that's just been robbed. Took me the better part of three years to figure it out and to trail them here. Here's how it went down.

"The widow Elliott would stick around town for one reason or another, and once the sheriff had returned with the posse, and the manhunt finally settled down, he would start sparkin' her.

Much to the pleasure of the town, the widow Elliott would take to his courtin' right off. After all, a married civic leader would be a good long-term prospect for the town, especially for a community that just had had a hard lesson on crime and on how important a lawman is."

"Some lawman," Al quipped, looking around for a spittoon.

"Throughout their whirlwind courtship the widow would constantly harp to whoever would listen about how much she missed home, or how her ex-husband had died because he went West, instead of staying back east where he belonged. So, once they got hitched the sheriff or deputy, or whatever he was being called at the time, would reluctantly have to resign his office."

"Let me guess," I interrupted. "Announcing his plan to return to the East in order to please his new bride. My God"—I shook my head in wonderment—"the town even threw 'em a going-away party."

"Wasn't the first time." Marcus added, "In fact, the lady's real name isn't even Elliott."

"What is it then?" Al asked.

"Bodine, same as his."

"His real wife?" I exclaimed. "No wonder she tried so hard to kill me." I paused to consider that. "By the way, thanks again for saving my life. Shooting a woman, no matter what the circumstances, has got to be hard." I extended my good arm toward the detective.

"Don't mention it," Marcus replied, shaking my hand.

"That all?" the doctor asked impatiently.

"Well, I always knew the pair would leave the town," Marcus continued, holding his finger up for the doctor to wait one minute, "but I didn't know where they had stashed the money, and I needed to know that, if I was to have any real proof. I thought maybe they might have handed it off to one of the other gang members, or perhaps buried it just outside of town. I didn't figure on them sitting right on top of the money. After each one of the robberies, the rest of the gang would then wait patiently until things quieted down, and then they'd leave town, one by one. Their excuse was usually financial woes from the bank robbery. The way I figure it, they'd all meet later at some predetermined location and divide up the spoils."

"And then they'd start all over again in a new town with nobody any the wiser," Al remarked, looking amazed.

"You should have been a detective," Marcus replied.

"I played one once," Al answered proudly.

"I've got to get started on this boy," the doctor insisted now.

I was still lying on the couch, but the odor of

camphor, alcohol, and other things in his office was beginning to make me dizzy. The doctor walked me over to his surgical table, and with the help of Al Kleiner and James Marcus lifted me onto it. He began dropping some nasty looking instruments into boiling water.

"Wait . . . please. Just one more second, Doc," I said. Turning to the detective, I asked: "You mentioned something about this being personal?"

Marcus's expression turned grim. His hand rested on the Bible for a moment as he took a long breath. "Time was when I once considered becoming an ordained minister. Then about four years ago, this bunch pulled a job in southern Colorado. At the time, Bodine was pretending to be an Army inspector with his men disguised as cavalrymen. They'd stolen their uniforms from an armory in Denver. The lone stranger they chose to frame for that particular job turned out to be a surveyor for a mining syndicate. He was a real nice kid with a bright future. Only twenty-five years old and the father of a two-month-old baby girl." He hesitated a moment. "They never did find the body."

"Go on," I encouraged. "How'd you find out about it?" I inquired.

"Friend of your'n?" Al asked.

Marcus shook his head slowly as tears formed in his eyes. "My younger brother."

"I'm truly sorry," I said sadly. "I know what it's like to lose kinfolk."

The detective looked up at the ceiling for a moment as if to collect his thoughts, and then took a deep breath. "Anyway, when he failed to write to his wife as he'd promised, she got worried, and asked me to investigate. From the descriptions the townsfolk gave me, the stranger, who supposedly robbed their bank, had to be my brother. Only I knew he was incapable of such an act. Eventually I joined a detective agency, and when I learned from their sources that there had been another robbery involving Army uniforms, I put two and two together. I started looking for similar crimes. My boss gave me free rein and I've been hunting them ever since. Problem up until now was finding them all in one place. There was no way to predict where they would go. Only the gang knew what town would be hit next."

"Must have been a hard journey," Al commented.

"The only real thread I had to go on was a very pretty woman that everyone always seemed to remember," he said.

"Hard not to remember her," I remarked.

"That was their one flaw. Men can blend in out here, but a women that good-looking can't. Eventually all I had to do was find her, in order to track the rest down."

"And that's why you came in on the same stage with her," I noted.

Marcus nodded. "I finally caught up with her in Abilene. Couldn't do much there, though."

"Why not?" Al asked. "Because you couldn't get anyone to help you?"

"Like I said, I didn't have any real evidence on them," he explained. "It was all supposition. No way to take them to court."

"Well, at least you won't have to worry about that any more," Al pointed out, referring to the lack of living defendants able to stand trial.

"An eye for an eye," the doctor remarked, sighing. He began threading some strands of silk on a long curved needle and grasped the needle in a scissor-like holder. He set that down and took out some sort of long metal probe. Finally he offered me a strap to bite on against the pain.

One look at that metal probe, and I knew I wasn't going to be the stoic type. I took the strap in my mouth.

"Seems like I recall there's something written in that book about the Good Lord finally getting retribution," Al remarked, pointing to Marcus's oversize Bible.

The detective nodded before answering. "There is," he replied, looking up, "but this time vengeance was mine."

EPILOGUE

My pa used to say that folks who claim money won't buy you happiness, probably never had any to begin with. Well, if money won't buy you happiness, it sure as hell can rent it for a while. At least that's what I'd have said if you'd asked me about it before I arrived at the town of Blue Lake Ridge. After leaving Bannock, in the Idaho Territory, I was riding high, flush with plenty of gold ore. There was more than enough to pay off the debt on my sister's ranch, with enough left over for a stake on a spread of my own. Funny thing is life often turns on a dime, and that little altercation I had in town had thrown all my plans right out the door. Little would describe it well enough if you can use that word to explain being flung off a cliff, dislocating a shoulder, spraining an ankle, bruising a few ribs, getting knocked on the head, and then later on getting shot in the same bad shoulder.

It took me the better part of six months to recuperate, time I spent divided between a remote cabin in the hills, playing poker with my friend Al, and week-ends in town at the Shuffle On Inn, with an increasingly attractive Millie. She was one girl who almost grabbed my heart for good.

One of the first things I did, after all the commotion settled down, was to have the local veterinarian check out my palomino. He seemed fine, but I wanted to be sure there were no ill effects from all the time he'd spent away from me.

I found the doctor nailing a new sign up over the old livery stable that now read: Dr. D. Malone, Veterinary Services and Livestock Boarding.

The vet climbed down from the ladder as I approached. "Like it?" he asked, removing a rag from his rear pocket and using it to wipe his hands.

"Looks good to me," I answered truthfully. "Wish you more luck than the previous owner had," I added.

"Didn't take much convincing to get him to sell," Dr. Malone commented. "Don't know what you said to him, but he seemed right eager to get out of town," he remarked.

"Oh, I just had a friendly word with him," I winked. "You know, to convince him how important a new veterinary clinic would be for the town."

The vet just stared back at me expressionless.

"So, how are things going?" I asked in an attempt to end the silence and to change the subject.

He looked down his nose at me, raised an eyebrow, and replied: "Better now that we finished all the remodeling. You here about the stallion?" he asked.

"That's right. So what's your verdict, Doc? How is he?"

"Doing all right I expect." Obviously he was a man of few words.

"So what do you really think of him?" I asked much as a proud parent would.

"Well, let me put it this way. If you were to sell him right now, I expect you'd get your money back." He stared back at me without cracking a smile.

"That's it?" I asked somewhat disappointed. I'd hoped for something more. I had bragging rights on him and found that most folks tended to admire that palomino.

"Pretty much," he answered. "Why?" He seemed puzzled.

"Oh, nothing," I replied shrugging. His bedside manner had dented my ego a little. "Thanks for the good word." I should have added: "Such as it is."

"Don't mention it."

As he returned to his work on his new clinic I had no doubt that he would end up a tremendous success, especially in a town like this.

I was glad to learn that the money my sister so desperately needed finally arrived, and happily for all involved it did so in time, much to the displeasure of the local Savings and Trust.

Unfortunately the remainder of my money seemed to just dwindle away over the weeks that followed. I learned that the biggest hole in the money pocket is the one on the top you keep reaching into. Some went for medical care, some for supplies, and more than a few coins were spent on local entertainment in town.

Normally, since my needs were relatively simple, all that spending of cash wouldn't really have amounted to a whole lot, but I felt indebted to my friend, Al, for having saved my life on more than one occasion. Against his wishes, I used up a good deal of my funds repairing his cabin and adding more livestock to his ranch. The rest I spent on a surprise gift for my new found best friend.

By his own admission Al Kleiner was an old, out-of-work actor content with his present surroundings, but although he made out as though it didn't really matter to him any more, I knew he secretly longed for the attention and applause only a stage can offer. That's why during one of my last trips to town I convinced the bank director that a growing town like Blue Lake Ridge was in dire need of a new theatre.

Seeing as how I was the one who had managed to recover the money his bank had lost, not to mention getting myself shot up in the process, the bank was more than willing to help. Besides, all the director really had to do was take the remainder of my gold plus the reward and then hold the balance of the mortgage on the property that we had in mind. Somehow bankers always seem to make out better than I do.

Like the saying goes, it's easier to make a horse thief out of an honest banker than an honest banker out of a horse thief.

Before long, I would leave town for good. But before I did I also had the local attorney draw up a contract making Al the managing partner of the Cracker Barrel Theatre, appropriately named after Al's little burro, in gratitude for her part in helping pull my fat from the fire. I didn't really expect any money back from all my efforts, but I figured it was cheap repayment for saving my life. I also hoped it would insure that my friend Al would be well taken care of. And you never know, maybe Al would turn out to be as good a businessman as he was an actor.

After some deliberation my new friend Detective James Marcus finally decided to stay in town. On the appointed day before I finally rode out I looked him up.

"If it ain't too personal, Jim, do you mind telling me if you're going to return to Bible study now that it's all over?" I asked.

He paused as if to consider his reply. "No, I don't think so. Too much blood on my hands. I think I'll stick with law enforcement for a while." He turned his coat lapel over to reveal a badge.

"After all, the town did need a new sheriff. Someone had to take the job."

"Looks like they found a good one," I commented. "But don't be too hard on yourself," I added. "After all, it ain't as if you took any blood from innocents. Hell they deserved what they got. Might not be too late to go back to the old life."

"Thanks, but you know things will never be the same as before. Besides, I seem to have a knack for this sort of thing. Who knows? Maybe it'll all work out."

"Well, then, I wish you luck." I rubbed my bad shoulder and, feeling somewhat embarrassed, added: "You know, I owe you my life for what you did here."

Marcus looked back at me. "No need to feel any obligation as far as I'm concerned. You're a good man and it was something that needed doing."

"Maybe so, but I'm still obliged," I said. I handed him a small card. "Here's my sister Judith's address, back home. She always seems to know how to find me. Honestly, you need any help, anytime, anywhere, you contact her and let her know what's up, and, I promise you, I'll come a-running."

"I do appreciate the offer, William," he said sincerely, "and the same goes for me."

We shook hands, and then he turned and walked

down the street headed I assumed for his new office.

During the time we spent together, I had begun to appreciate his quiet courage, good nature, and intelligent conversation. I felt a little disappointed that we wouldn't have more time to ride the river. But as Uncle Jake always said: *You never know when paths will cross.*

"*Vaya con Dios*," I said quietly to myself as I turned the stallion and rode away.

Maybe someday I would return to Blue Lake Ridge and who knows, maybe Al could turn a profit on my investment. Truthfully I didn't really care. I was alive, back on my palomino stallion, and riding out to do what I knew best: looking for mischief out in the high and yonder.

ODE TO THE COWBOY

In the American West a man's brand is his
  pride
Its more than a mark to place on a hide
When you ride for the brand you're loyal
  and true
Working all day for the wages you're due
You stick through the bad as well as the
  good
And protect your own as Americans should
A brand would be nothing without a good
  hand
But our country has many throughout the
  land
Together they strive and together they toil
Those of the towns and those of the soil
In work they find grace, courage and pride
Tired perhaps but proud to have tried
While others, founder, fail or just quit
They prove themselves daily men of true
  grit
Their reward is in doing and daring to try
Staring their enemies square in the eye
Let others seek glory, riches or fame
America's cowboys still honor her name

Books are produced in the United States using U.S.-based materials

Books are printed using a revolutionary new process called THINKtech™ that lowers energy usage by 70% and increases overall quality

Books are durable and flexible because of Smyth-sewing

Paper is sourced using environmentally responsible foresting methods and the paper is acid-free

Center Point Large Print
600 Brooks Road / PO Box 1
Thorndike, ME 04986-0001 USA

(207) 568-3717

US & Canada:
1 800 929-9108
www.centerpointlargeprint.com